ADVANCE PRAISE

"Justin Hunter is the real goddamn deal. *Leaving Arizona* is one of the best new collections of minimalist fiction I've read in years. Like its title, this book is sweltering, and brutal, and a sort of cross-your-fingers hopeful that proves why hope can be as dangerous as despair. Read this book. Follow Justin Hunter. Seriously, do it. Don't be a fool."

— Nick Gregorio,
author of *With a Difference* and *Good Grief*

"Justin Hunter's blistering vision of the southwest and its people—abused, desperate, in love—is both unforgiving and suffused with empathy. A compelling and harrowing debut."

— Stephanie Feldman,
author of *The Angel of Losses*

"A haunting depiction of young children using drug needles as darts, of someone searching for meaning in the seasons and a female killer, shedding layers of her life daily, like a snake. Hunter's stories bring you to the heat of the action and dart away oh-so-soon."

— Isabelle Kenyon,
Managing Director of Fly on the Wall Press

"Justin Hunter's full-length collection of twenty-six pieces of short fiction, *Leaving Arizona*, includes an array of characters whose lives are as undernourished as the desert that hems them in. Filled with great writing and great characters, each story will leave the reader thirsty for more. This stripped-bare prose packs a punch. Not a word is wasted."

— Christopher P. Mooney,
author of *Whisky for Breakfast*

LEAVING ARIZONA

In the sky, the clouds slipped past the moon, and the desert shed its darkness for a moment. Infertile land that gave us just enough to survive. An offering. A chance. But it would never be enough. Nothing would ever be enough.

*

{from 'Galaxie Under the Stars'}

LEAVING ARIZONA

stories

Justin Hunter

Rhythm & Bones Press
Trauma-turned-Art

Rhythm & Bones Press
Birdsboro, Pennsylvania

Leaving Arizona
© 2020 Justin Hunter
© 2020 Rhythm & Bones Press

Interior & Cover Design: Tianna G. Hansen
ISBN: 978-1-952050-02-2
First Edition May 2020

www.rhythmnbone.com/leaving-arizona

Content Warning:
Much of this work deals with difficult subjects including sexual assault, child abuse, violence, and the darker nature of humans. Please take care while reading.

CONTENTS

COUNTING SEASONS

My body's down there. Right beneath me. Six feet, give or take a few inches. But I'm here, above it. Suspended. I can see three hundred and sixty degrees around me, but I can't get away. I was able to escape once, but now I'm not sure that will happen again.

There's not much snow in the winter. Not here. But when it does come, the cold blackens my toes. The flakes slice at skin that's not there. Morning frost clings to my lips, and icicles form along my nails. In the summer, my skin bubbles. It reddens, bakes, and bursts. In the summer, I wish there were trees to hide the sun.

Through it all, I can't move. I can't go out and discover who I am. I can't search for the person who caused this. I wish I could remember what happened to me, but all I remember is my body. The first time I was stuck.

The first time, I was there for months. I watched my skin fall away from muscle and bone. My body was half-covered by a tarp in the middle of the desert. I could see the world going on around me, but I wasn't part of it. The animals came. They gnawed. They ate. And I watched, unable to stop them. Unable to move.

Until he found me. The boy with the blonde, curly hair. The boy who didn't want to see my body but didn't leave me there. When he found me, I could move. I followed him when he told his parents. I followed his parents when they called the police. I followed the police when they came to collect my body. I followed the detective when she tried to identify me and the sketch artist when he attempted to draw me, reinvent my skin. I followed the medical examiner when he loaded me into a cheap coffin. I followed the state employee who drove me out here.

And now I'm stuck again.

They stopped trying to find me. They still don't know who I am. They gave up. They don't know who did what to me. I'm just a body, buried in a state cemetery with a headstone that doesn't have a name.

Now I watch the seasons. I used to count days, but there are too many of those. Four is a nice number. I count seasons. I've seen each season three times from this spot.

There's a mesquite tree that's missing a branch now because of the last summer storm. Lightning hit it, snapped the branch, left the tree scorched. There's a tall saguaro with arms that have begun to sag since I first got here. There's the hole to a rattlesnake den not far from my grave. I wonder if the snake is down here with me.

Sometimes I make up names for myself. While I watch the sun slide across the sky, I think I might have a plain, common name. Other times, beneath the moon, I think I'm unique. No one would have my name but me.

I just want to know who I am, who I was. Then I'll be free.

I watch the hawks high above me. They circle. They dive. They eat and leave. Back to their homes. I watch them fly until I can't see them anymore, and I imagine I'm with them. Soaring away from this place.

Someone will solve the mystery of me. Of who I am. I don't know exactly what happens when they do, but I know I'll be free. Someone will start searching again. I'll stop being forgotten. I'll get my name. I'll get my story. But for now, I'll count the seasons.

ARMY MEN

I prick my hand on something under the sofa. When I pull my hand back, I expect to see blood, but there is none. I press my head to the floor, nose poking under the torn base of the microfiber sofa, and I see it. Right there next to my yellow, foam rocket—the one Lyle said wasn't under there. It's a needle. Not the kind you sew with, I think. It's a different kind. I pull it out and show Lyle.

We both sit in the middle of the living room and stare at it. I place the needle on the floor in front of me, and it settles between the thick, brown threads of carpet. My brother, being six, thinks it's the coolest thing in the world but doesn't know what to do with it. I've got five years on him, so I know exactly what we should do.

"Let's throw it at the wall like a dart."

"Won't Mom be mad at the hole?"

"It'll be a small hole. Plus, Mom sleeps most of the day, she'll never see it."

"What about—" Lyle stops, but I know what he's going to ask. He forgets sometimes. I don't need to tell him Dad's not coming home. He figures it out on his own then moves on.

Turns out, needles don't fly like darts. We can't get it to stick into the wall, so Lyle says we should use it as a squirt gun. I tell him that's a stupid idea. We decide to fill it with water and inject the barrel cactus Mom keeps on the front porch.

Tina comes up the dirt driveway while we're pumping the cactus full of water. She winks at Lyle then messes up my hair.

"How you doing, Jack?" she asks.

"My name's Jackson."

Tina holds her hand up in front of her, shrugs, then walks into the house.

"I like her," Lyle says.

"Why?"

"I don't know."

"She's just a babysitter."

Lyle takes the needle from me, shoots water across the porch, and giggles. "She's always here when Mom's here. And you said you don't need a babysitter."

I leave Lyle to keep playing with the needle and go inside to make lunch. Tina is talking to Mom in the back bedroom. Mom's voice sounds like it's underwater, or like she's talking too slow. I stop trying to listen and think about last night.

She came out of her room in the middle of the night. I heard the television and saw her sitting on the couch, staring at the screen. I sat in the hall and pretended I was watching the show with her.

Sometimes, she comes and lays on the floor in my room or Lyle's room. When she does, she makes noises in her sleep, kicks like a dog, but I don't wake her. I'm not sure she slept at all last night, though.

I make a couple sandwiches for Lyle and me, then I make a few more for school tomorrow. They gave us lunch cards after Dad died, but I hate the food they serve at school. I throw the sandwiches in plastic bags, slide them into paper lunch sacks, toss in a couple apples, and put it all in the fridge.

I start to pull open the front door to tell Lyle to come eat, but I stop when I hear Tina.

"He's coming later for the money," she says from the back bedroom. "You got it, right?"

Before my mom can respond, I hear a thud. Tina laughs, and I sneak through the living room and peer down the hall. Tina is leaning against the wall Mom started painting a few months ago but never finished. She's half-sitting, half-standing. She smiles at me before standing straight and walking past me toward the kitchen. She comes back with a spoon and goes into Mom's room again.

"I can't spot you this time," Tina says before shutting the door.

I find Lyle in the backyard—a collection of weeds, dead grass, unfilled holes from the time we had dogs, and old car parts my dad used to collect.

"Jackson, I put it with its friends." Lyle smiles at me. "They're army men coming to attack our house."

I cross the yard to the pile of dirt he's standing near, ignoring his salute. "What're you talking about?"

"Look." He points to the top of the dirt pile. I follow his red-skinned arm—I need to get him some sunscreen—and I see the needles. Ten of them, standing straight up.

"Where'd you find them?"

"They were here," Lyle says. "In the hole. I stood them up and stuck them in the dirt."

I tell him to stop being dumb, to grow up. Then, I drag him toward the house. He tells me he doesn't want lunch, he doesn't want to go inside with me. He asks if he can play with his friend Jaime.

"No," I say. "Jaime lives too far down the street."

Lyle punches me in the arm and tries to kick away, but I hold him. I want to get mad, but the way his eyebrows crease and his lips stretch tight reminds me of Dad. So, I don't say anything, and we go inside to eat.

*

Mom tries to cook dinner for us later that night, but she doesn't make it past the sofa. She's too sick, and I tell her that's alright. Lyle tries to get her to play cars on the living room floor, but she stumbles back to her room instead and falls asleep.

Tina brought over a couple frozen dinners when she came by earlier—chicken nuggets and pudding. I guess she's not all bad. She likes to joke with us, sometimes she shows me how to answer a question on my homework, but mostly she's in the back room with Mom.

I help Lyle scoot his chair in at the wooden table. When Dad bought it, the table was smooth, polished. Now, it's dented and covered with crayon and crusted food.

"Did you get the mail?" I ask Lyle.

"No mail on Sundays, dummy."

I throw a nugget at him. "From yesterday, stupid."

He nods while shoveling pudding into his mouth, nuggets untouched.

"Eat your chicken."

"Mom wouldn't make me."

"Yes, she would. Just eat the chicken, Lyle."

The orange of the sunset slides down the wall near the side window until we're in the shadows. I flip on the light and remember the three days we went without power. I don't know what she does with it half the time, but Mom has money. The military gave it to her, but she forgets things sometimes. Like the bills.

"My face hurts," Lyle says.

"Yeah? Well, it's killing me." The light against Lyle's sunburned skin makes him glow orange.

Lyle laughs like he always does when I make that joke, then narrows his eyes. "I'm serious. I want Mamma to put some of that stuff on me."

"The green stuff?"

He nods and takes a bite of chicken. His pudding is gone.

"I'll get it."

I walk through the living room toward the hall when someone knocks on the door. I look at the door, waiting. It's a heavy door, made from an old oak, Dad always told me. It's got two windows toward the top, but I can't quite see out of them. Some of the kids at school are two or three inches taller than me.

I pull the purple curtains away from the living room window and look toward the porch. I can't see the man's face because of shadows cast by his cowboy hat, but I see the gun on his hip. The man knocks again. I start to head back to the bedroom to hide, but I see Lyle standing in the entryway to the kitchen, looking at me, expecting me to handle it.

I suck in as deep a breath as I can and open the door. The man looks like he's been left in a smoker too long. His brown skin matches his eyes. His black mustache wraps around the edge of his mouth and twitches as he moves his lips. He nods his head and touches the brim of his black Stetson before walking into our kitchen, past Lyle.

Lyle holds my waist. "He's a cowboy."

"No he isn't."

"Look at him."

"He's not a cowboy."

His plaid shirt is tucked into faded blue jeans. His black and red cowboy boots ride halfway up his calf.

He is a cowboy.

The man walks back into the living room, winks, then heads down the hall. His boots disappear first, somehow. I follow him, just enough to see him go into Mom's room. Something breaks in her room, and Lyle grabs my shirt, tugging, trying to get me back to the living room. But I watch.

"This is a start, but I'll need more," the man says.

"More what?" Lyle asks.

"Money," I say, eyes fixed on the doorway to Mom's room.

"I've got some."

"Not your change."

"It's not change, it's money."

"It ain't enough," I say.

When the man leaves Mom's room, I fall back into the living room. Lyle falls behind me. I lift him up and we stand by the couch as the man walks across our living room toward the door, crumpled twenty-dollar bills in his hand. He tips his hat once more and is gone.

Lyle sits on the couch and asks how cowboys make money. I ignore him and go down the hall. I look inside the room, expecting something—I'm not sure what, but something. Mom's asleep on the floor next to the bed.

When I get back to the living room, Lyle asks if I want to play Nerf guns.

I do.

*

By the end of the week, Tina is yelling. The day after the cowboy came, she didn't yell. Or the next day. But now, she's yelling.

Lyle and I just got home from school, and we're sitting in the kitchen. I hear Tina say something about cracking open the trust fund. About making sure they're covered. I try to ignore it and make a peanut butter sandwich, no jelly.

Lyle colors on the table. I should get him paper, but I don't.

Mom missed a parent-teacher conference today at school, but I told the teacher it's because she had to work, reminded the teacher about Dad. I hate doing that, but I've had to a lot more lately. I don't want strangers asking about my mom.

"We should go outside," I say.

Lyle keeps coloring, so I grab him by the arm and pull him toward the back door. "Stop, Jackson. I was coloring."

"I know, but we don't need to hang around inside all the time."

In the backyard, Lyle walks to his needle army and reorganizes them. The sun has already fallen behind the mountains, but there's enough light to last us a while.

If I stayed inside, I'd listen. I'd try to understand things that I don't want to understand. Out here, I can just play.

I pick up an old soccer ball, but it's flat. I drop-kick it across the yard, over Lyle's head. He chases it but stops, looking down the side yard toward the front of the house.

"What?"

"There's a truck," he says.

I come stand by him and see the pickup. A gray Dodge Ram with a cattle guard. I can't see who's in it, but I can see the person get out. Whoever it is disappears down the walkway toward the front door.

I run to the back door and stand with my back against the wall just to the side. I lean over enough to see inside, through the kitchen and toward the front door. Lyle stands in front of the back door, in plain sight. I pull him behind me.

The front door swings open, and the cowboy walks in. At first, he stands in the doorway, hat pulled low on his head, gun tucked in his holster. Then, Tina appears in the living room. She holds her hands out in front of her and says something I can't hear.

The man smiles, then slaps Tina. She falls to the floor and holds her arms in front of her face. The man picks her up, slams the front door, and presses Tina against it.

"Stop!" she yells.

He doesn't raise his voice enough for me to hear, but I can tell he's angry. He places his forearm against Tina's throat and she starts coughing.

Lyle tries to slide past me to see, but I hold him in place.

"What is it?"

"Quiet."

Tina's face turns red. The man removes his forearm from her neck and draws his gun. He places it against her forehead and says something.

"She'll get it," Tina yells. "She's got money."

The man starts to walk toward the hall, but Tina grabs his arm. He pushes her back against the wall, shoves the gun against her temple. He pulls back the hammer.

Tina presses her hands into her pockets and pulls out a wad of cash. She hands it to the man, who holsters his gun. He steps back, counts. He nods, points down the hall, tips his hat.

When the man leaves, Tina falls to the floor again, crying.

I run to the side yard, and Lyle follows. I get there in time to hear the door slam and see the truck drive away. When we return to the back door, Tina's gone.

I walk into the kitchen with Lyle on my heels. We sit at the table and listen. Tina's talking to Mom. She's crying and yelling. She says she's not coming back here. She says Mom is on her own.

I ball my fist. Mom's not on her own. She's got us.

Tina doesn't look back when she leaves. The house rattles when the door slams shut.

"What happened?" Lyle asks.

"Nothing."

He shrugs, then starts coloring on the table again.

*

Two days later, the cowboy is back.

"*Buenas noches*," he says as he walks through the door.

I back away and give him room.

"Is your mother back there?" He nods toward the hall, and I wonder how his hat stays on his head. His shirt is darker but just as plaid.

I shrug, but Lyle says, "Yes, she's back there."

The man smiles and wipes his mustache like he's trying to flatten it.

"Who are you?" I ask.

"Me?" He smiles. "I'm nobody."

Before he left for Iraq, Dad told me I had two jobs. I had to protect my little brother and I had to protect Mom. If I didn't feel right, he told me, I should call the police. I don't feel right. Like when I took my first at-bat during Little League, shaky and sick.

The man doesn't go to Mom's room. He walks into the kitchen, circles the table, looks at each chair. He taps the top of one of the chairs—the one near the fridge—and slides it out. He sits down then places his cowboy hat upside down on the table.

I follow and sit across from him. "You shouldn't be here."

Lyle stands close to the table and reaches for the man's hat, stretching his arm and lifting himself on tiptoes. I smack his hand away.

The man laughs and Lyle laughs, too.

"I like you boys," the man says. "Family is important, no? But you're right. I shouldn't be here. Yet, I am. And I need to speak with your mother."

"She's sick," I say.

"I'm sure she is."

"She is," Lyle says, climbing into the chair next to me. "She sleeps and throws up a lot."

The man nods, slides the gun from the holster on his belt. He pushes something and the magazine falls out just like it does on my pellet gun. He flicks a bullet out of the magazine with his thumb, sets the bullet in the middle of the table, slides the magazine back into the gun, and holsters it.

"I'm leaving this with you." The man taps the table near the bullet. "I want you to watch it. Make sure it stays here. We wouldn't want it ending up anywhere else, would we?"

Lyle shakes his head.

The man stands and looks me in the eyes. "Your mother needs help, boys. But I'm not the one to help her."

He walks back into the living room. I hear him in the hall. At first, the knock on Mom's door is soft, but I don't hear her open it. Then, a boom. It sounds like wood breaking, like when I snap mesquite branches across the concrete porch out front.

"Is Mamma all right?" Lyle asks.

I ignore him and look at the phone on the wall. Lyle and I called 911 a couple years ago, just to see what it was like. I wanted to show Lyle what a real policeman looked like, so we called and asked for one to come. The officer that came to our door sat us down when he realized nothing was wrong, and told us not to call again.

But I think I should call. It's different this time.

I stand and grab the phone.

"What are you doing?"

I put my finger to my lips and tell Lyle to keep it down. I can't hear the man anymore, so I start to hang up, then there's a thud against a wall in the back of the house. I think I hear Mom cry. Then, a slap.

I dial.

The voice on the other end of the phone asks what my emergency is, and I whisper about the man in our house. I give our address and hang up.

"The police are coming," I tell Lyle.

He frowns like he does right before he forces a cry, so I go to the fridge. I grab a Yoo-hoo and toss it to him.

"It'll be alright," I say.

There's another crash from Mom's room. Lyle tells me to go check on her, and I know I should. But I don't.

A minute later, the man is back in the kitchen. He picks up the bullet from the table, slides it into his pocket, winks at us. "Your mother understands now."

"He called the police," Lyle says, pointing at me.

I shove Lyle's chair so hard he nearly tips over. I look up at the man who has narrowed his eyes. His eyebrows look thicker, shading his entire face. He rubs the handle of his gun, then grabs his hat.

"I wish you hadn't done that." He places the hat on his head and touches the brim with a slight nod. "Enjoy your night, *niños*."

The man leaves and shuts the front door behind him. I walk into the living room and pass photos of Dad on the wall, some with him in uniform, some without. I pass the sofa and walk down the hall. I stop outside Mom's room and take a deep breath. Lyle is right behind me, but I don't turn around. Mom's door is open, splintered pieces of the door frame on the ground. We go in.

The nightstands are flipped on their sides. Mom's jewelry box is smashed on the floor. The sheets are crumpled next to the bed, and all the pillows are torn open, stuffing dusting the carpet like that time a few years ago when it snowed.

Mom is crying in her bed.

*

It didn't take the police long to get there, but we're not waiting on them anymore. Lyle and I are back on the sofa, waiting for someone else.

He taps me on the elbow. "Do you think I can get the other soldiers and put them outside tomorrow?"

"What soldiers?"

"The ones from Mom's room."

"Sure."

Mom stayed in her room while we waited for the police, said she needed to clean up. I didn't see how she was going to clean the bruise on her face, but Lyle and I went to the living room anyway. When the police came, they took Mom out of the house with her hands behind her back.

She screamed for us. Lyle screamed too, but I held him close.

Now, Lyle's holding Mom and Dad's wedding photo. The police officer who spoke to us earlier is in the kitchen talking to other officers. We're supposed to wait for someone to come talk to us, to take us somewhere else, to pass us off to some family member I can't remember in a state we've never been to.

Lyle frowns. "I want Mamma."

"I know."

I tap him on the shoulder until he looks up at me.

"Does your face hurt?"

He nods.

"Well, it's killing me."

Lyle fights back a laugh, then his face cracks. He sets the photo down and hugs me. I hug him back and don't let go.

SHEDDING

It was the last hotel before the border. I probably shouldn't have stopped, but they wouldn't catch up to me until tomorrow. Not in this skin. It was still fresh.

I'd told the man at the front desk my name was Karen, but he knew I was lying. I couldn't just tell him Carmen Pascuela was checking in. Couldn't pay with anything traceable. So, Karen it was. And cash it was. Sometimes, the names come before I need to use them. Not this time. This one was spontaneous, grown from exhaustion and the dimming creativity that comes with trying to be someone else while always carrying your original self.

Now, I'm standing in front of the mirror in the bedroom. Not the bathroom mirror. I don't like the lighting in there. The bedroom mirror sits on the dresser and leans against the wall. The television is just to the right of it. Off.

For a minute, I look at my hands in the mirror. The blood is gone, but I can still see hints of red. Or, I think I can. It's been months— no, years. There's nothing there, but I can see it. Like when I made Kool-Aid by myself as a kid. Streaks along the knuckles, down to the wrists. I pull my hands away from the mirror and can't see red anymore. But it'll always be there.

Just like that first skin. That first life. The one that had me running back and forth across the border. The one that had me meeting men like Manny. The one that forced me to end men like Manny.

The phone in the room rings.

I don't pick it up.

It rings again, and I answer this time. "Hello?"

No one says anything.

"Hello?" I repeat.

Nothing.

I'll try something different. "*¿Hola?*"

After a few seconds, a man's cheery voice says, "*Bueno.*"

Then the phone goes dead.

I return to the mirror. I shouldn't have stopped, but I need rest. It was a long drive from Denver. I cut west then south to hide my tracks. Through Arizona, down toward Yuma. Home, I think. I always come back home. Or through it. Criss-crossing west with a pile of used skins trailing behind me, memories of people who never really existed billowing from the tail pipe of whatever car I managed to get my hands on. On my way through Yuma, I passed the dunes and wondered what it would be like to lay in that ocean of heat and let the sand blow across my body until I couldn't be found.

That's what I should have done with Manny. Maybe then, I'd still be Carmen Pascuela.

One last look. Remember this skin. It's not special. It doesn't hold memories worth saving. But I need to remember. If only so I don't try to use it again. If I forget, I might forget the life that happened to the skin. Like the life that happened before this skin—the one that led to this. I can't forget that. I need to know why I have to keep shedding.

My mind is a notebook and Karen's life has been written across its lines. Stamped. Noted and locked away. Just like the others. Pamela was around long enough to have lived through two boyfriends. Lia managed to get work at a dollar store in Utah. Beatrice had the least money and lived on the street.

All pages in the notebook. All reminders of why Carmen Pascuela can never come back. Why Carmen Pascuela had to die.

And yet, the phone call, here in this hotel room, proves I have to keep shedding. They'll never stop. But neither will I. The pages in my mind's notebook of lives is limitless.

DIRT ROADS

Kyle pulled the cigarette from his lips and hid it behind his back as the red Toyota Camry skidded through the dirt driveway and stopped in front of the trailer. He dropped the cigarette and kicked it off the concrete porch, out of sight. He waited to see who was driving.

The passenger window on the Camry rolled down, and Garrett leaned across the passenger seat. His long, brown hair snaked out beneath his blue Dodgers cap.

"What the fuck, man?" Kyle asked.

"You coming or what?"

"Is this your mom's car?"

"Let's go." Garrett adjusted the side mirror, sat up straighter in the seat.

A couple weeks before, Kyle offered to let Garrett drive the shit can—Kyle's rusted Volkswagen Beetle—but Garrett wouldn't go near it. Said he just barely got his permit and didn't want to mess around.

Kyle leaned against the wood beam holding up the awning above the porch and smiled down at Garrett. "I dunno. Not sure I trust you driving me around."

"Come on, man." Garrett looked at him, then sighed. "Please."

Kyle thought about dragging it out longer, but fuck it. If Garrett was driving his mom's car without a license, there had to be a good reason.

Kyle jumped off the porch and checked around back to make sure his mom wasn't doing that thing she did. Staring at the mountains in the distance for hours, past the sage and palo verde dotting the land behind the doublewide. She wasn't back there, so Kyle climbed into the passenger seat.

"Finally got your license?" Kyle pulled his seatbelt on and slid a crushed pack of Marlboro Reds from his pocket.

"Nope." Garrett dragged the shifter into drive.

Dirt spun up behind them. Kyle rolled up the window to keep from choking on dust. Plus, he was wearing his new Jordans. Sure, he hadn't paid for them, but they were still expensive.

Garrett took the dirt roads like they did in the go-cart he and Kyle built together in fifth grade. Garrett was new in town back then, and Kyle hadn't been able to keep friends too long. He'd do something stupid and their parents would think he was a bad influence. The end. It went on like that until he met Garrett.

The go-cart lasted them the entire summer before the steering column snapped, sending Garrett into a saguaro. That summer proved to Kyle what a real friend was. Every time Kyle messed up— the fire he lit behind Garrett's house, the broken windows at the elementary school, the shoplifting—Garrett stuck around. Garrett made the friendship last, telling his parents Kyle wasn't all bad. That he always deserved another chance.

The Camry slid around turns, missing the dirt embankments bordering the makeshift road by inches.

"What's up?" Kyle asked.

Garrett gripped the wheel with both hands. "Nothing," he said. "Just a drive. Practicing."

"Since you scared the shit out of me back there, mind if I light another?" Kyle held up his pack of cigarettes.

"Doesn't matter."

Kyle lit his cigarette just as Garrett found paved road. The Camry's tires chirped as Garrett made a hard left at the intersection. Kyle saw the deputy sitting in his parked cruiser on the side of the road, dome light on even though it was ten in the morning and the sun shone through bright blue sky. "Shit, slow down, man."

Garrett eased off the gas. He checked the rearview, but Kyle had seen the deputy looking down at paperwork. He wasn't looking to pull anyone over this morning. Kyle wondered if his dad might make that transition one day. Move from corrections to patrol. A lot of guys did it. Of course, that was before the thing happened at county last year. Kyle's old man promised he had nothing to do with it, but Kyle didn't figure the Sheriff's Office would be taking any CO's anytime soon.

Kyle didn't care where they were going. Looked like maybe the interstate, but it didn't matter. It was something to do on a Saturday. Something to keep him from doing something else. Garrett was good like that. He was the type of friend who kept you from being you.

Don't ever forget how good a thing that is, Kyle reminded himself. You as you, doesn't work. The you with Garrett is passable.

Yet in moments of stupidity, moments of frustration, Kyle wondered why he ever hung out with someone like Garrett. It was easy to get angry at an obstacle, even if that obstacle prevented Kyle from doing something dumb. Like the time last summer when Garrett took a punch from Kyle because he'd kept Kyle from fighting someone else. Garrett didn't fight back, didn't take a swing at Kyle despite his bloody nose.

"Are we calling this learning time?" Kyle asked after a long draw on his cigarette. "Hours behind the wheel? I mean, I know I've had my license for a whole year, but I ain't exactly the best person to learn from."

"I don't care, man. It's just driving."

Kyle shrugged. "What's up with you?"

They came to a four-way stop and Kyle looked out the window. He caught a glimpse of a black and brown javelina. It stared at them, deciding whether or not to charge. Before it could make a decision, Garrett pulled away. Kyle imagined the javelina chasing them until its lungs gave out.

It was quiet until they hit the interstate. Then Garrett said, "I hit Davey."

"Davey Brintz?"

"You know any other Davey's?" They passed the last exit in town—if you could even consider it part of town. Most people who lived closer to the city certainly didn't.

"Alright, calm down. What about Davey now?"

Garrett squeezed the steering wheel until his knuckles went white. "I'm not just driving for practice, Kyle."

"I know."

"I hit him."

"So you hit him," Kyle said. "Not exactly your style, but so what?"

Kyle thought they'd head north, but Garrett took the exit for Interstate 8 west. Garrett finally looked at Kyle. "You don't get it. I hit him, man."

"Oh shit, you mean, like, with your mom's car?"

"No, my fist."

Kyle stared out his window for a while, trying to make sense of it. He understood Garrett was scared. The kid had never gotten in a fight his whole life, and now he had. It was normal to be scared, but they had gone from simple-joyride to stolen-car-on-the-run scared.

Garrett was six-three, two hundred pounds. He shouldn't be afraid of anything. He should be playing football. Maybe he could get himself a scholarship if he did. Then he'd be able to get away from the jokes, get away from the town. But Garrett didn't want any of that.

"Help me understand this, Gar. You hit Davey Brintz. Why?"

"He said something about Kas."

That pinch in Kyle's neck came back like it did every time he heard her name. He knew Kas wasn't the type he could go with. He did things. She didn't. That didn't stop the feeling Kyle got.

"What could he have possibly said about her?" The exits stopped coming so frequently, replaced by barbed wire fences skirting ranches that no one seemed to own. The Camry slipped between the jagged rocks of hillsides blown apart by dynamite decades ago.

"Said she tasted like pineapple," Garrett said.

Kyle laughed. "I'm sorry, but come on. Was he saying he was kissing her and her mouth tasted like pineapple? Because if so, fuck him. Kas wouldn't touch that motherfucker. And don't even tell me he was talking about the other."

Garrett nodded. "He did mean the other, man. Said it to my face. He said, 'Kas tasted real good down there. Like pineapple.'"

That was the type of thing you don't say about a guy's girlfriend. Hitting Davey in the face was fair game, and Kyle was glad Garrett had done it.

"You know Davey's full of shit, right? Kas wouldn't touch him. Shit, you and Kas are so straight, the whole world knows you're both waiting for marriage. You probably close your eyes when you take a piss just to make sure you don't see your own dick. And I'm pretty sure Kas's pops sewed her panties straight into her skin."

Garrett didn't laugh.

Kyle snuck a look at the speedometer. They weren't going too fast yet, but Garrett was pushing it. Each time Garrett got upset, he pressed the accelerator down a little harder.

"I'm just messing with you. Davey Brintz is a fucking asshole. He deserved to get hit."

"Yeah, but I killed him, man." Garrett clenched and unclenched his jaw.

Kyle laughed. "Sure you did. You punched him and now he's dead. Got it."

"I'm serious," Garrett said. He checked the rearview mirror then looked over his shoulder. "Fuck, fuck, fuck."

"What?" Kyle spun in his seat and saw the light bar flashing red and blue. He got that feeling in his stomach. It didn't matter that he hadn't done anything this time. It was like the first time he got busted for shoplifting. Picked up in the damn parking lot. He hadn't even made it home with his score. His gut dropped like it did then.

Garrett pressed down on the accelerator as Kyle said, "It's just Border Patrol. You're good, man."

Garrett let off the gas and leaned back in his seat. The white and green SUV passed them on the left, lights on but no siren. "Shit."

Kyle watched Garrett breathe for a minute. His breathing went from quick and shallow to slow and deep. "What was that?"

"I fucking told you, Kyle."

"You didn't kill Davey. It's not possible. You probably just knocked him out."

Garrett shook his head then beat his hands against the wheel. "You didn't see it, man. He's dead."

"OK, tell me about it then."

"I hit him too hard. He went down with one punch."

"You're a big guy, you should be proud of that punch."

"No."

"Why do you think he's dead?"

Garrett rolled down the windows. The warm air spun around them, slapped at Kyle's ears, tugged on Garrett's hair. He took a deep breath, looked at Kyle for a second, then back to the road.

"Davey's head hit the curb when he went down. We were down on Cholla Street, in front of his house. I only hit him once when he said what he said. That's it."

"Listen, man. If you saw his lights go out, it just means he's knocked out. You don't have to worry."

"He's more than knocked out. You'd know if you had seen his head."

"What do you mean?" Kyle lit another cigarette.

"Right here." Garrett ran a finger from his temple down to his cheekbone. "The entire side of Davey's head hit the curb. His fucking eye socket caved in."

"Jesus."

"Blood started coming out his eye, his nose, his ear, and I just fucking ran."

"Still, you don't know he's dead. They probably took him to UMC. They were able to save that guy after he fell from the sixth floor of the that hotel downtown last year. They'll fix Davey up, no problem."

Kyle wasn't sure he believed that.

Garrett lifted the ballcap off his head, ran a hand through sweaty hair, then pulled the cap low across his brow. "He stopped breathing after he hit the curb. It was instant. He hit and he was dead."

Kyle watched the mountains rise and fall on the horizon in step with the rhythm of the road. Like the desert was taking a nap, breathing in and out gently. Garrett hadn't said it, but Kyle understood what they were doing now. "Why the hell are you driving west? We live less than an hour from the Mexican border. You're going to run? You run south."

"So you think I should?"

"You already are, man. But I'm not sure where you're trying to run to."

"California. The beach. You're coming, right?"

"You should turn around, head back. We'll figure this out."

Garrett shook his head and kept driving.

Kyle could go to California. He wondered if there was anything really holding him back. His mom barely spoke anymore, and when she did it came out all wrong, mixed up. He asked his dad to take her somewhere because of it, but he was too busy. He was pulling double shifts, not because they needed the money—mortgage on the trailer was paid. No, his old man worked doubles because he liked being at work more than he liked being home.

Garrett didn't have much holding him back either. After his dad finished his overnight at the mine, he worked part-time at the high school, coaching girls' soccer. Kids at school all said the same thing: Garrett's dad would get off from the mine then get off on watching high school girls kick balls around. Then there was Garrett's mom. She volunteered at the mission on the reservation. She was an Indian lover, she'd gone native. Everyone at school said it, but Garrett never seemed to mind. In reality, there was only so much someone could shoulder. It was no wonder Garrett snapped on Davey.

All this time, Kyle had propped himself up on Garrett, but Garrett didn't have anyone to lean against. You're a piece of shit, Kyle thought.

"You can't run to California."

Garrett shook his head. "Well, I ain't going to Mexico."

"You think a seventeen-year-old kid with no money can make it on the run?"

"We can make it together."

They came up on a rest stop, but Garrett didn't slow down. "If Davey's dead, you know they'll pick you up the first time you land on a security camera. First time you leave a fucking fingerprint anywhere."

"No way," Garrett said. "Never had my fingerprints taken."

"You never had your prints taken? Are you fucking kidding me? What about sixth grade. Mrs. Lettle's class. The D.A.R.E. cop took all our prints."

"That was just for fun. To show us what it was like."

"Where do you think those prints end up? It was their chance to get us on record. My old man took my prints the minute he started working county. Difference there was he didn't lie about what he was doing. Told me he wanted to find my dumb ass the minute I fucked up."

Garrett made a noise like he was clearing his throat to speak. He rolled up the windows and turned on the A.C.

"Well I can't go back. I killed someone—"

"What about Kas, huh?"

"I don't know. What'd she do with Davey? Why'd Davey say that?"

"He's an asshole. Kas didn't do anything with him. I promise you."

Garrett squeezed his eyes shut longer than Kyle was comfortable with. When he opened them, he said, "I couldn't shake the thought of it. His fucking mouth on her down there. I just swung. Didn't think."

"Welcome to my world, buddy."

Only Garrett wasn't in Kyle's world. Garrett should be back home, applying to college and finishing school. He and Kas should be getting ready to go to some college far away. The only shot Garrett had was to turn around and face it all.

If that didn't work, Kyle didn't know what would happen.

They rode in silence for a long time. Kyle spotted the sign for the next rest stop ten miles away. "Hey man, I have to take a piss. Let's hit that rest stop."

"No way, we can't stop."

"Garrett, no one is on you now. Hell, I'm not sure anyone would ever know you did this. We can afford a fucking piss break."

"Alright, damnit."

At the rest stop, Garrett stayed in the Camry while Kyle got out. Kyle didn't need to go, but he went into the bathroom anyway. Standing in front of the faded mirror covered in graffiti, he wondered what it would look like to be on the right side for a change. He thought about playing video games in Garrett's house, playing basketball in the park. Then he thought about every time Garrett kept him from doing something he shouldn't. The car he almost broke into, the fight he didn't end up having, the meth he wanted to try but didn't because Garrett flushed it.

Kyle ran the water in the sink, but didn't wash his hands. He listened to the sound of it hitting the metal basin. He needed Garrett to turn around and head home. That wouldn't happen if Kyle rode with him to California.

Back out by the car, Kyle leaned in through the window. The sun was high and his shadow stretched across the roof. Garrett had given up on the hat, and it hung across the top of the shifter.

"Let's go back," Kyle said.

"What? No. I can't." Garrett searched his face. "You're leaving me?"

"No, I'm not. We just need to head back. Like I said, I'm not even sure the police will know it was you. How would they?"

"They'll find out. Or Kas will. Someone will know what I did to Davey."

"If they're going to find out, they'll find out with or without you there. At least if you're there, you can tell your side. Get out in front of it."

"No, fuck that."

Kyle started to reach in to pull Garrett from the car, but stopped. "I can't go with you to California. That's it, so let's head back home and figure this out. Show me Davey's actually dead, and we'll figure it out."

Garrett spun the Dodgers cap around on the shifter. He mopped his head with the back of his hand. Tapped the steering wheel. He turned to Kyle and shook his head. "I would have been there for you, man. You know that."

"I am here—" Kyle slipped off the side of the car as Garrett threw it in reverse and backed out of the parking spot, kicking up gravel.

Garrett sped off without looking back. Kyle stood in the middle of the lot and watched the Camry disappear on the horizon. He kicked at the gravel before walking back to the sidewalk and sitting down. He stared out at the freeway, watching the cars pass by, each one a second ticking away. Distancing himself from Garrett, from Davey, from the life he'd known.

NOT FRIENDS

Nick hit the side of the mountain at sixty-five miles an hour.

We rode our motorcycles up Catalina Highway earlier in the day, rising eight thousand feet above the desert floor. We did what we'd been doing for the past three months—parked at the lookout point and pulled cans of air freshener spray from my backpack. I stole them from the grocery store where we both worked overnight. We shook them, placed the nozzles in our mouths, and inhaled.

I liked to wait until the blood vessels in my brain crystallized and my mouth tasted like menthol. Nick said he was ready when the clouds circled his eyes. We raced down a floating mountain, wondering if we could soar from the road to the valley below. The tar and painted stripes below my tires would stretch and roll and reach up from the ground, slapping at my handlebars.

Nick's bike was faster than mine. He always reminded me of this, and that always reminded me of how Nick and I weren't friends.

Friends were something you needed when you died. Something my sister needed so she could say her funeral was a success. All those people, crying over her, talking about her life.

Friends were about remembering. I rode with Nick so I could forget. We rode south to the University of Arizona's campus, cutting down the bike paths whistling at girls walking back to their dorms. We rode to the gates of the Air Force base and blew kisses to the guards. We rode north to Casa Grande to see if we could hit two hundred miles per hour on the highway.

But we weren't friends.

The first time Nick asked me to grab a can of air freshener, he told me he'd been up for thirty hours straight. When I asked why, he shrugged. But while riding the mountain with my brain a frozen crystal ball, I understood why Nick would go two days without sleep. Sleep was a trick that let you drift. Awake, you were anchored to a moment.

With three turns left before the bottom, I leaned to my left, my knee an inch from the ground as I locked my wrists and kept my handlebars steady.

Nick didn't lean.

When I passed him, I didn't see Nick. I saw colors painted against the mountain. Orange, white, red.

I reached the valley and rode west toward my house. I came in through the garage, tossed my bag on the bed, and flipped on the television.

I expected to see news coverage of Nick's rescue. Lights, police, Nick's old high school photos pasted on the screen.

But there was nothing. No reports. No mention of the crash.

I opened my bag and pulled out the last can of air freshener, shook it, and placed the nozzle in my mouth. Nick and I were never friends, anyway.

SHOTGUN SIGNS

The movie theater played classics on Tuesdays for two bucks a pop. You had to get there before eleven, though. And they wouldn't serve alcohol even though the goddamn bar was just as stocked in the morning as it was late at night. So, Daryl poured some coconut rum into a plastic bottle of Coke while still in the parking lot. He found the rum tucked in the bottom drawer of the dresser at the old motel he stayed at last night. He slid the bottle into his jeans pocket when he walked into the theater. Now, he was itching to pull it out as he waited for the 10:30am showing of *The Jerk* to start.

His daughter's first movie had been in a theater like this. Small, empty, playing classics like this one. Dani laughed and laughed and *What's Up Doc?* carried them through to the black-screen credits.

That was before Daryl decided he didn't want his daughter anymore.

An usher walked past Daryl, looking down. Suspecting. Then, he came back and stood next to Daryl. "Sir, is everything all right?"

Daryl kept his eyes on the screen, waiting for the movie. "What?"

"You don't look well."

"I'm not."

"Can I do—do you need anything?"

"I need plenty."

The lights dimmed and the usher gave up and walked away. Daryl pulled the rum and Coke back out and sipped as the movie began.

He wished he could say he was drunk when Steve Martin danced on the porch of that house at the end of the movie. But he didn't feel a thing. He stood, knees popping, and walked out of the theater, past the concession stands, and into the parking lot where the sun had begun to bake the tar.

He stood in the middle of the road before walking to his truck, and tried to hold the sun's gaze. His eyes burned after a second, and his eyelids shut after two. He used to tell his daughter staring at the sun would make her blind, but that was when Dani was just a girl. Now, he didn't know what he'd tell her.

When Daryl got to his truck, he tossed the empty Coke bottle in the bed. The bottle of coconut rum in the glove compartment should get him through his day of driving. Johanna used to drink stuff like that. Bay Breezes made with Malibu, Hurricanes made with some other shit that tasted more like Kool-Aid than alcohol. She spent her summers sipping cocktails on the back porch, pretending it wasn't a hundred and fifteen degrees outside.

He and Johanna were still married as far as the law was concerned. But she wasn't going to find anyone new with the way she was, and Daryl didn't want anyone in his life. Except, now, he wanted Dani. Wanted to tell her he'd been wrong, he'd made a mistake.

He climbed into the cab of his truck and started it up. Most days began like this now. Maybe not with a movie, but with a couple of drinks and too many memories.

Dani had been eighteen when she told them she was moving in with Sharon. Johanna told her it was a great idea, told her she supported it. And that's why Daryl's wife still got to see their daughter.

Daryl shut his eyes and tried to remember the exact words he'd said to Dani. "Ain't no daughter of mine shacking up with a dyke." That was it.

Of course, if it had stopped there, he might not be driving up and down empty highways of Southern Arizona to keep from going insane. No, Daryl told his daughter she was a piece of shit. Human garbage. That if she left his and Johanna's home, there'd be no coming back.

She left, and now all he wanted was for Dani to come back.

But there wasn't anywhere to come back to. Daryl'd been living out of his truck and cheap motels for months since Johanna's thing at work. Somehow, the way Daryl treated their daughter didn't do them in. It was something that happened on the job. From what she told him, Johanna had to use her gun and it messed with her head.

He guided the truck onto the back road leading toward the state highway cutting west toward Tucson. Dani was living in a trailer with that same girl across the state line up in Utah. They must have wanted to escape the desert. He couldn't blame them.

Daryl had driven up there once or twice. Long drive. He'd sat in the bed of his truck, drinking warm beer and watching the light through the curtains of the trailer's windows. He couldn't go knock on the door. He'd tried to come back from what he'd done, but Dani wouldn't allow it.

A cloud streaked in front of the sun, dropping Daryl into shadow. When the cloud passed and the sun lit the cab again, its light caught the edge of a piece of chrome on the passenger side floorboard. He leaned over and pulled back a rust-covered tarp and looked at the shotgun on the floor. The old 10-gauge wouldn't do much in its current state, but it helped Daryl sleep at night.

Sometimes, just before laying his head back in the reclined driver's seat of the pickup at the end of the day, Daryl slid the shotgun barrel between his lips, careful not to smack it against his teeth. He held his thumb on the trigger, and he closed his eyes and thought. Sometimes about Dani—like how he didn't care who she fucked now, probably didn't care back then either. Sometimes about Johanna—how he missed her forgiving him for everything he'd ever done as they fell into bed together.

And on these nights when Daryl let his tongue run along the cold steel barrel, he let his brain wander until he couldn't stand it anymore. Then he pulled the trigger.

The dry click of an empty chamber made his blood go cold and his skin tingle.

He purchased the shotgun at a gun show after he got tired of passing road signs torn apart by birdshot. If people loved shooting up metal signs on the side of the highway, he might as well give it a try. But he never got around to buying shells.

When Daryl made it to Interstate 10, he went south then caught Interstate 19 toward Mexico. He ducked off I-19 at the first state highway he could find and set the cruise control. Yesterday, he drove five hundred miles back and forth across Pima County, Santa Cruz County, and Cochise County. He hit a coyote in the last hour of driving, and that told him it was time to call it a night.

By one in the afternoon, Daryl was fifty miles outside the city. He passed trailers and ranches. A fireworks stand stood a few yards off the highway. When Dani was twelve, Daryl tried to impress her with a fireworks show on the Fourth in their backyard. Johanna had told him not to do it, but she had gone to work when he sat Dani in a lawn chair out back. He lit the first firework without any trouble. The second one, though, exploded on the ground and caught Daryl's arm on fire. He put it out with just a few burns, but Dani cried the rest of the night.

He'd take that night over any other he'd had in the last few years.

How he'd made it this long was a mystery. Dani was thirty now, had two kids she adopted. That Sharon girl—woman, now—worked at some crisis management company. Didn't make much as far Daryl knew since they were still stuck in that trailer. But Johanna told him their daughter seemed happy.

For the first couple years after Daryl told Dani not to come back, he stayed angry. Couldn't look at a picture of her without wanting to hit a wall. He'd shattered every picture of his daughter lined up on the dresser after Dani moved out.

Daryl spun off the cap on the rum, took a drink from the bottle, then closed it. He watched a storm build to the south. All show, no go. The clouds puffed and darkened, but when it came down to action, the storm would back off. Like a bully forced to fight for the first time.

Daryl had been fighting for some time. Fighting himself. Fighting Johanna. Fighting pain after he got hurt on the job. He broke his back in six spots when that wall came down on him. Now, Daryl wasn't supposed to lift anything heavier than ten pounds. He was supposed to take Vicodin to numb the pain. And he was living off the settlement the company gave him.

That happened four years ago. Maybe that's what changed his mind. Made him realize what a piece of shit he was. Or maybe it was Johanna leaving him.

The first time Daryl tried to apologize to Dani, to beg her to let him back in, was three years after she left. Johanna gave him Dani's number and Daryl called. Sharon answered and even begged Dani to come to the phone, but Daryl heard his daughter in the background.

"I ain't got a daddy," she'd said to Sharon. Then the phone went dead.

Daryl tried once more after the accident at work. From his hospital bed, he scratched out a letter. Said he wasn't worth the time she was taking to read the letter, but he hoped she could forgive him. Said he loved her. Said he might even love Sharon if Dani would give him another shot. He wrote about his own father. No excuse, he'd told her, but his own daddy hated everything. Hate flowed through bloodlines, but Daryl should've been better.

When he got an envelope back from Dani, his heart about stopped. He was out of the hospital by then, laying on the couch at home. He tore it open and found his original letter shredded. He dumped the tiny pieces of paper to the floor, laid his head on the couch, and closed his eyes. He hadn't tried to reach out since.

Daryl passed a few trailers, some slump block homes, a gas station serving as a grocery store, and a post office. He watched the hawks high in the sky, circling, waiting. Waves of heat rose from the tar ahead. He imagined rain coming, cooling the road. He passed the shell of a burnt-out car and an old mattress tossed to the side of the road.

Then, he passed a gun store and hit the brakes.

Daryl pulled off the road and looked at the store in his rearview mirror. It was staring back at him, daring him to break eye contact. He threw the truck in park and stepped out into the dusty hard clay lining the highway.

He walked back to the store and pulled open the door. An old Indian with close-cropped hair nodded then went back to watching daytime television on the black and white mounted behind the counter.

"You got 10-gauge shells?" Daryl asked.

The Indian didn't look up, but he pointed at a wall toward the back.

Daryl looked at the rifles on racks along the wall, the handguns under the glass. He could look all day, but he wouldn't be able to walk out with one of those guns until passing the background check, and that would take too goddamn long.

He picked up a box of 10-gauge Remingtons from the shelf along the wall in the back and walked up to the counter. It smelled like sawdust and whiskey in the shop, and reminded Daryl of working out in the garage when Dani was little. He built her a rocking horse from wood he'd picked up in the neighborhood. She watched him, clapping when each new piece was finished. And he got that thing polished to a shine while he drank cheap booze from a styrofoam cup.

"What're you drinking back there?"

The Indian looked up. "What?"

"Smells like something I'd drink."

The Indian shook his head. "You're on the reservation, so you assume we're all drinking, all the time. That it?"

Daryl shook his head and placed the shells on the counter. "Nope, just smells like whiskey. That's all."

"Well, you smell like rum."

Daryl shrugged and pointed at the box of shells. "How much?"

"I'm not selling these to you when you're drunk."

"I ain't drunk."

"Well, you're not right either."

Daryl shook his head. "Just sell me the damn shells."

The Indian looked Daryl in the eyes. "Anything else you want to say to me? Maybe you want to ask me to do a rain dance for you, huh?"

Daryl thought about the storm building to the south. The Indian went back to watching the television. Daryl pulled out his wallet. He grabbed a twenty and laid it on the counter. "I didn't mean no offense. This should cover the shells."

Daryl grabbed the box, but the Indian slammed his hand down on Daryl's hand. "Watch your mouth next time."

Daryl nodded and slid his hand and the shells out from under the Indian's hand. When Daryl was back outside, he opened the case and looked inside as if he was worried he'd just bought an empty cardboard box. He found five rounds stacked in a line inside. Satisfied, he closed the lid and walked back to the truck.

He should have been angry. And maybe he would have been in the past. Maybe he would have been if he were still at home feeling sorry for himself. Or, maybe that old Indian made some sense.

Daryl drove on for another twenty or so miles. He drove until he stopped seeing homes. When he was surrounded by saguaros and mesquite trees and open desert, he searched for a road sign. He found a sign warning drivers that the bridge ahead would ice before the road. He couldn't remember the last time it iced anywhere around here.

He pulled to the side ten feet from the sign. Daryl lifted the shotgun to his lap, grabbed the box of shells, and climbed out of the truck. He went to the tailgate and popped it open. He slid the shotgun into the bed and set the shells on the side rail. Daryl climbed up, feeling his back try to pull apart as he did.

He picked the shotgun back up and grabbed the shells. Up front at the cab of the truck, he laid the 10-gauge down across the roof and opened the box of shells. He'd seen Johanna clean and load her guns a million times, but she never wanted Daryl to have one of his own.

That's why he kept his daddy's old bolt-action at the job site, tucked under a ventilation duct. Until the accident. He never did get that thing back.

When he and Johanna got married, she'd been out of the Air Force for six months. She didn't know what to do next, and Daryl suggested she try to catch on with the sheriff's department. And after all that time, she was still there.

Daryl loaded a round into the shotgun and held the gun across the top of the cab. He aimed for the sign in front of the truck, squinting under the late afternoon sun. He laid his finger alongside the trigger and sucked in hot air coming off the top of the sheet metal.

When he was young, Daryl's family had big get togethers. They didn't have a name or a reason for them, but his grandparents had a lot of kids and those kids had kids. He could remember driving from Arizona out to New Mexico with his parents and pulling into the dirt lot of the ranch house. There'd already be six or seven other cars there, and when they'd get inside, the house would be an echo that wouldn't end. Laughter, shouting, cheering, crying. All of it rolled into one.

He'd taken that away from Dani. He didn't think before he spoke, didn't even think before he thought. Daryl squeezed the trigger.

The birdshot tore a hole in the top left of the sign, but he knew about half the pellets went sailing past the sign, cutting through humid air. He looked out to the south and the storm clouds getting darker. Getting closer. He loaded another shell.

Daryl started thinking about where he might sleep tonight. He figured he'd be best sleeping in the truck, but if the storm hit, he'd prefer a real roof over his head. He took aim at the sign again, but stopped. He laid the shotgun on the roof of the cab and wondered what Dani would be doing right about then.

Daryl realized he didn't know what she did for work. Didn't know what she did for fun. He made a decision years ago—one that he couldn't understand anymore. He just said things, spoke too much. Didn't listen enough.

After a moment, Daryl slid the remaining shells from the box and tossed the box into the brush off the side of the road. He counted three shells in his hand, rolled them back and forth. Then he threw them to the side, leaving the one chambered in the gun. He climbed down from the bed with the gun leaning against his shoulder.

He wondered if Dani would have come to the funeral if that wall had killed him. Probably not. He wouldn't go to his own funeral even if they had an open bar.

Daryl climbed into the truck, laid the shotgun on the passenger side floorboard, and cranked the engine. He watched the storm swirl overhead and heard the first rumble of thunder. The storm might have a little go in it after all.

He put the truck in gear then flipped a U-turn in the middle of the highway. It was a half-day drive up to Dani's trailer in Utah, and he wanted to get as far away from that storm as he could.

HOW TO BE A MAN

When he was born, you told your wife—told yourself—you'd teach him to be a man. A real man, not the kind on the cover of magazines or the kind you hear about in bars. Through his wails, you whispered.

"I'll always be there. I'll always help you."

You watched him grow from a baby into a toddler, defiant and angry. Watched him learn to run, to climb things he shouldn't be climbing. Watched him learn to speak, learn to say no. You held him when he fell, kissed him when he didn't want to go to bed. You watched him become a person, no longer this alien creature you had to mold into a human. He was you, only smaller, better.

You rewarded him when he was good, sent him to his room when he was bad. That time he stole Halloween candy from the bucket before bed, you took away his favorite Ninja Turtles toy. You still feel bad that you forgot to give it back, but you did it for the right reason. To teach him. To help him one day become a man.

You played baseball with him out front when he got older, watched him throw a fit when he struck out. You taught him that success was what he defined, not other people. And he understood.

Three days after his eleventh birthday, you stood on the neighbor's front porch, telling him he better be sincere.

"We get one chance to right a wrong," you told him. "One chance to come back."

You watched him apologize for throwing rocks at the neighbor's cat, but you didn't see the sincerity. You let it slide. He was just a boy. Just did something dumb.

"Boys," you said to the neighbor. "I don't know what gets into their heads."

You and the neighbor shared a laugh, shook hands, righted the wrong. Your son saw you leading by example. You were a man, teaching him to be a man. Always do what's right.

You watched him breeze through math in junior high, told your wife he was going to be a whiz. Going to be a scientist. Maybe he'd go to Notre Dame, get a full ride. You told her he'd be at the top of his class when he finished high school.

But he wasn't. You got the calls from the office. He'd skipped again. He was on academic probation. You found him drinking one of your beers in his room late one night, and you tore into him. You yelled, you threatened. You did everything your father had done with you, because goddamnit, maybe you weren't teaching him how to be a man after all. Maybe you didn't know a damn thing. Maybe you needed to do what you never wanted to do.

And it worked. He went back to school, brought his grades up, finished high school with a B average. You'd done your job. Maybe he didn't get that scholarship. Maybe he wasn't going to Notre Dame or NYU or anywhere else. But he made it through high school, and he knew right from wrong.

He lived at home. He didn't need college, and that was alright because you'd seen what he was growing into. Something good. You'd seen him with his girlfriends. He respected them. Held the door for them. Never pushed himself on them. He was a man.

You saw him with his friends. They talked politics and poverty and social issues. They wanted to change the world. It didn't matter none of them had jobs at twenty. Didn't matter none of them went to school.

They were men. He was a man. You'd done your job.

And then last night, he came to you, blood on his white t-shirt. Crying. He'd done something, couldn't tell you what. But he did tell you. He was tired of not having money. He was tired of sitting around and talking. He was tired of the world getting what it wanted while he let it pass him by. He broke into the big house two blocks over—the one with the Audi parked out front and the Navigator in the garage. He'd gone for the jewelry, but he didn't know the owner was home. Didn't know the owner had a gun. He reacted with the gun he brought along.

But you didn't know where he'd gotten a gun. From his friends, maybe. Or the gun show. Didn't matter. He had it.

He shot that man in the chest. Watched that man die. And now he was crying into your shoulder, telling you he didn't want to go to jail.

And you were crying. You didn't want him to go to jail. You didn't want to think about that man, that man's family, the blood, the bullet. You just wanted to look your son in his eyes and tell him you loved him. He'd made a mistake, but you loved him. You didn't want him to go away.

You packed him a bag, kissed your wife. Told her you had to run an errand. You helped him change into clean clothes, kept the bloody shirt and dirty jeans. You loaded him into the front seat of your truck, and you drove.

You flashed your passport at the Nogales border crossing, waited. Looked at your son. You nudged him and handed his passport out the window as well. Two minutes later, you were in Mexico. Thirty minutes later, you were lost. You handed him his bag, told him to go. Told him you loved him. Kissed him on the top of his head.

When he climbed out of the truck, he cried. He walked. And you left.

On the drive home, you thought about men. Men don't run. They stand up for what's right. You taught him that. You taught him to be a man. But you didn't care about him being a man that night.

All you cared about was him being your son.

LEAVING ARIZONA

Rather than a note, the missing boy left a scorpion in his sister's bed. To be fair, it was a dead one. Of course, she wouldn't know that as she pulled back her comforter and screamed. And the missing boy wouldn't be there to laugh and poke fun. But it happened nonetheless. And it gave Arizona something to hate him for. Something other than the real thing she should hate him for.

This was before the missing boy was missing, but once he left, he saw the news report. He saw his mother crying on the television screen, her mascara running down her face, her eyes bloodshot. No one knew that's what her eyes looked like all the time, that her makeup was smeared across her face so often he wondered if she knew how to apply it.

"Find my baby," she said on that first newscast. "I miss him and want him home."

Sure, she did. She wanted the missing boy to come home, to go back to what he once was. He remembered seeing Arizona in the background of the shot, head down. She looked fine, she was fine. She'd be all right without him.

She'd gone twelve years living in a state that shared her name. That alone brought the type of torment that would thicken her skin, prepare her for a life without her brother.

Those reporters, they couldn't believe her name. "Arizona? And you live here, in Arizona?"

They didn't know Mom thought it was funny. Didn't know Dad had wanted to call her Charlene. All those reporters knew was my sister was a novelty who would play well on television and in newspaper articles.

The missing boy remembered the one quote Arizona had given to the newspaper—the small one that had headquarters up on the northwest side of town.

"My brother doesn't deserve to come home."

It made the front page in bold typeface. The missing boy almost walked right past the paper laying on the bus bench when he saw it, not realizing it was his sister who'd said such a thing.

But she was right.

He rolled over in his dusty sleeping bag and lifted the rock off the newspaper he'd stolen from Pap the day before. He unfolded the paper and laid it across the warm caliche. He flipped through its pages, but the coverage of his disappearance had faded. He was a vague memory, a shadow fading from a wall.

The missing boy rose, folded the newspaper again, slid it into the back pocket of his last pair of jeans. He rolled his sleeping bag, tied it off, and slung it over his shoulder. The clearing he'd slept in the last couple days was a few hundred yards off the freeway. He'd caught up with Pap, an old man who sold papers, and found out about the camp. A few homeless people in tents and sleeping bags, hiding from police roundups. It was a damn miracle that the missing boy found Pap. In the month he'd been out there, he'd discovered he didn't enjoy sleeping alone. Especially when the coyotes started to yip and the scorpions started rustling in the brush.

He yawned and looked east. The sun gripped the top of the Catalinas. He shielded his eyes to watch orange and yellow melt away the purple horizon. A perfect day to make his real escape. Today, he'd hop the Union Pacific west. Today, he'd be gone for good.

"You out?" Pap asked.

The missing boy nodded, still staring at the Catalinas, wondering if he'd ever see something as beautiful in all his life. It didn't matter. Beauty couldn't wrap arms around him, pull him close, hide him away from the next thing to come.

"Going for the train today."

"That right?" Pap climbed all the way out of his tent, his Wildcats championship shirt hanging down to his knees.

"Yes, sir."

"'Bout time, huh?"

"I been saving."

"Nah, you been stalling."

The missing boy had thirty-two dollars in his back pocket. It had taken him the whole month since he left to make that money. Wasn't much, but he had it, and he'd make it last the whole way through to California. It was only a half-day ride on the train. Better than going north or east where he might have to hop off one train, get on another. No, California was the only place that made sense.

"I'm not stalling anymore. That night train going west is mine."

Pap shook loose a jar of instant coffee from a bag he kept in his tent. He poured a pinch of the nasty, black granules into a dirty mug then grabbed a jug of water. He filled the cup, swirled it, took a drink. "You caught a train before?"

The missing boy shook his head.

"Not that easy, my friend. Especially for a kid."

"I'm not a kid."

"Since when is a middle schooler not a kid?"

"I'm fourteen, a high schooler. Not a kid."

"Right," Pap said. "What I'm saying is be careful."

The last cigarette the missing boy's mother put out on his arm bubbled the skin just above the fold of his elbow. He thought about that before responding. He thought about the last bottle of Jack she'd thrown at his head. He thought about the day his father showed up on the steps of their trailer three years ago, promising he'd take the boy and Arizona away. And he thought about the sound of his father's shitty Harley Davidson riding away in the middle of the night.

"A train isn't shit."

"Still." Pap took another sip of coffee then offered the missing boy a straight blade sheathed in cloth.

The missing boy shook his head. "I can't take that."

"You can, and you will, 'less you want to see that money you saved taken right out your pocket."

He took the knife and thanked Pap. Then the missing boy set out toward the Union Pacific rail station south of downtown Tucson. It would be a couple hours walking, but he had time. He'd get there early to scout the right car. He'd heard about Border Patrol and sheriff deputies crawling the yard, looking for train hoppers. Give yourself time to watch for them, he thought.

As he walked, he thought about the trailer, about his sister. Worst case, he figured, Arizona was being ignored. Their mother put in five or six hours a day at a place she called The Clubhouse. Really, it was a cowboy bar two miles from their trailer.

The missing boy wondered why their mom chose him. He didn't know why Arizona got a pass. He was happy for her, but he didn't get it. He was old enough to remember the first time their father left, and maybe that was it. He was the "man of the house." He was the reminder of his mother's choices. That night when he and Arizona's father came back then left, his mother beat him worse than he'd ever gotten it before.

Without realizing it, he stopped walking. The paths cutting through the desert led in every direction—a homeless freeway system amongst cacti and sage. He tried to force himself forward. Just pick a path and head for downtown. But Arizona's voice knocked around his ear drums.

"She'll keep getting worse," Arizona said a couple months before the missing boy left.

They'd watched their mother polish off a bottle of something new, something cheap. She couldn't afford the Jack by then. "She'll be all right," he'd told his sister.

Their mother hadn't always been like that. Without the missing boy around, she'd get better. She'd never raised her voice, never laid a hand on him or Arizona before their father left. But after, she took up that job at the bar and something broke inside her. She was the Thanksgiving wishbone that held together until she couldn't anymore, until she snapped.

She couldn't get worse. If she did, the missing boy didn't know about his sister, didn't know how she'd hold up. But he was the cause, not Arizona. Without him there, his sister would be fine.

Yet, he started walking back south, back toward the dirt lots that held groups of trailers parked side by side with nothing but mesquite and the beating sun as a backdrop. He'd just take a look. No one would see him, and he'd be back on his way to the train once he saw that Arizona was alright.

It was funny to think about his disappearance. The desert surrounding the trailer, for about a mile in every direction, was crawling with police and volunteers. Maybe he had run away, but they had to assume he'd been taken. His mother pulled out all the stops to get her punching bag back. Tears, pleas, missing boy posters. But they didn't look far enough out. The guys at the camp figured out who he was, but no one said anything. Not to each other and certainly not to anyone outside the camp.

Pap had tried to convince him to go home that first day when they met, told him living out in the desert wasn't a life at all. Pap had said, "Your life back home can't be much worse than this."

The missing boy pulled up his shirt and showed Pap the scars, the bruises that had yet to fade, and the old man shut right up.

He made good time as he neared the dirt road leading toward the lot his mother's trailer sat on. But the closer he got, the slower he walked. He remembered a time two or three years ago when Arizona tried to do something. It was one of those fall days that still felt like summer, and the missing boy had been sweating through his shirt. Everyone had been sweating. His mother cooled off with whiskey on the rocks, and when she was feeling nice and cool, she decided her boy was looking a little too comfortable. A little too relaxed and lazy, a little too much like his father. She dragged him into the one bathroom they all shared in the trailer, told him to clean the bowl.

"What about gloves?" he'd asked. The inside of the bowl was crusted in brown and black God-knows-what.

"Gloves?" his mother asked. "You don't appreciate anything I do for you. I'm sick of you thinking you're hot shit. You are nothing. You can go right the fuck out that front door and go live with him."

"Maybe I will," he said.

His mother grabbed him by the hair and shoved his head into the toilet bowl. She pushed until his face was pressed up against the inside of the bowl. "Clean it, now."

Arizona came into the bathroom crying. "Stop it, please, Mom."

Their mother didn't hit her, didn't yell. Instead, she calmly told Arizona she was in charge and she needed to watch him clean that toilet with his bare hands. Arizona shook as she leaned against the wall watching. He remembered her tears dripping onto the chipped linoleum floor.

The missing boy picked up his pace, ignoring the memories, ignoring the pain that crept through his bones as he thought of his mother.

When he saw the trailer, he stopped again. He had a thought that he'd had many times over the last month. He wondered if he loved his mother. Yes, he had to. No amount of beating and yelling allowed a boy to cast his mother aside. He couldn't stop loving her, but he could be selfish. He could set out on his own.

But he loved his sister too, and he'd check on Arizona one last time before he went.

Arizona had never felt their mother's bony knuckles against her cheeks, never felt the cold tines of a fork turn hot as they jabbed into her triceps. She never felt any of it, and she never would.

Except, he wasn't sure. As he inched closer to the trailer, he'd grown sure of something else. He'd grown sure that he couldn't be sure about a damn thing after he left.

The missing boy stayed missing by pretending he knew what he was doing, by pretending to have a plan. But he didn't know shit. The first week on his own, if he let himself remember it accurately, was terrifying. He'd almost been picked up by police for taking a piss in public, but he ran into the desert and disappeared. He'd been bitten by a lizard while he slept, and he dreamt it was a Gila monster, jaw clamped down, injecting its poison into his body for all eternity. He had been kicked and pushed when he begged for money near the I-19/I-10 interchange.

There was a time when things with their mom started spinning out of control and he tried to convince Arizona to run. Not with him. Alone, just her. He didn't want her to see it, didn't want her to be part of their mother's destruction. He knew what their mother did to them would stick with Arizona. The endless stream of cigarette smoke choking off the outside world. It would suck away Arizona's potential.

She told him back then, "I'd never leave you."

The words still tore at his chest, a constant reminder of who he was. Now, it was him who had run and left his sister alone. But she was going to be fine. He'd see that now.

The missing boy made it to the rear of the trailer, the cracked clay crunching beneath his feet. He wiped his nose, ran his fingers along his moist cheeks. He saw his mother first. She stood in the kitchen with a cigarette between the skeletal fingers of her left hand, and she had an empty glass in her right. She'd been beautiful once. He remembered the way she looked when she would go to his school functions as a boy. He stood outside the window, transforming his mother back into that woman. The smile, the laugh, the smooth hands that could fix anything.

Arizona stepped out of the shadows in the kitchen. Her face was bruised, her eyes welling with tears. The missing boy almost ducked out of view, but he had to see her. He had to know what he'd done before he could fix it.

He'd convinced himself that, somehow, Arizona would be fine. He was just like his father. A coward who would run rather than stand up. He would change that now.

Arizona opened her mouth to say something to their mother, but their mother lifted the glass in the air and threw it across the room. It hit Arizona in the stomach, and she doubled over, crying and cursing and praying.

"God isn't here to help any of us right now, so you keep his name out your mouth," their mother yelled.

Arizona slid to the floor and hung her head between her knees. Her back rose and fell with sobs as their mother watched. The missing boy slipped down from the window and sat in the dirt. All the words, all the things his mother had done to him, all of it fell on Arizona now.

"I give you a roof, girl. I give you food. The least you can do for me is get me some fucking cigarettes. You know how hard it is for me to drive. I'm not asking much."

He couldn't see them anymore, but he knew what was happening. Their mother would be crossing the kitchen and leaning over Arizona's shaking body like she had done to him so many times. She'd force feed guilt until she was sure you hated yourself. Then, she lay down the insults.

"You think you're better than your mother," he heard her say. "You're a whore just waiting to spread your legs. One day, you'll come crawling back to me, alone with a couple kids to raise. And you'll know. You'll wish you had listened to me. Treated me better."

Then there would be the slap. The missing boy listened through his own sobs. It came a few seconds later. Then Arizona's scream. He felt it all. He lived it all. He remembered the first time his mother hit him. It had surprised him so much he didn't feel the sting of her hand. He didn't cry. He apologized in that moment. And he apologized for years after.

He grabbed his knees and begged himself to act. To do something. But his stomach burned and his eyes remained shut. All he could do was listen.

"Get your ass up," his mother yelled. "Go get me some cigarettes before I give you something else to cry about."

He couldn't hear Arizona's response, but he knew she'd said something because his mother raised her voice louder.

"What? They won't ask for ID at the gas station down the road. Don't give me your bullshit excuses."

His sister could be saved. She could be removed from that trailer. The missing boy could take her along on the train to California. But he'd have to go inside.

He listened as his mother slapped Arizona again. He stood as the yelling grew louder. He could go in, but he was already inside that trailer. He'd always been there. Leaving didn't change that. He'd never get out.

Unless he left.

The pain in his bones surged, stretched, clawed at his muscles. It seized his body and sent him back to the dirt beneath the trailer. He sat there begging himself to be strong. To ignore the pain. To do something right for once.

Through his tears, he watched a scorpion sneak out from beneath the creosote shrub to his left. It scattered into the open dirt and clay and stopped, confused. The missing boy took out the knife Pap had given him, held it flat in his hands. He told himself he was strong enough, but that was just another thing he didn't know shit about. Strength.

Before the scorpion could rush back into the safety of shrub, the missing boy slammed the knife through its body, pinning it to the desert floor. He knew what he should do, what the right thing was.

But he was already crawling away, his knees and forearms shuffling and kicking up dust. When the pain in his bones faded, he stood. He walked away from his mother. Walked away from Arizona. And the further he got from the trailer, the less he hurt. All he'd have to do was forget his sister, forget what he'd done.

He walked all the way to the rail station near downtown. He waited for the train to take him away. He would forever be the missing boy, but he'd never again be the hurting boy.

His sister would have to make her own way.

Strip Mining

Sonia's desert was a pit, carved into the clay where saguaro and sage once reigned. A hole in the ground where everything had once been. Where nothing was now.

Sonia's desert was a reminder that anything could be taken. Permission not needed. The things that made it the desert, the things beneath the dust, were pulled away. Stripped without a thought beyond the pleasure of the moment. The pleasure of taking something away.

Sonia's desert wasn't a desert anymore. It was just a pit, and Sonia considered throwing herself in. But she would move on. She would escape.

Somewhere. Someday.

JUMP

The bracelet came off yesterday. They give you the option of keeping it on for fifteen bucks a month. Constant monitoring to protect you from you. If not for the costs of monitoring, they'd probably require everyone wear one forever at no charge. But if I kept the bracelet on, I wouldn't be able to cash in. The last three years would have been a waste.

Every kid was required to wear a bracelet until they were eighteen. The bracelet monitored heart rate and chemical balances. It was a poor attempt to keep kids alive on this life path. The bracelets were connected to emergency services, and when alerted, police and EMS on the streets and in the schools would respond to a person who'd injected themselves. It was pointless. The emergency services personnel and their backpacks full of drugs to help bring someone back almost never worked. They had to get to someone within the first minute of Jump being injected to have a chance.

And no one would be getting to me when I sent that brown liquid rocketing through my veins tonight.

Now that it was off, it was time to visit Mel. She'd release me, let me correct the mistake that sent my father to prison when I was just a kid. But I needed to do something else first.

I picked up my cell phone and checked the time. Just past eight. Curfew in less than an hour. I'd try to squeeze in dinner with Eddie, even though he'd made his feelings clear.

He answered on the third ring. "Hey, Tyler."

"Eddie," I said, but I didn't know what to say after.

"I'm sorry about the other day, it's just…"

I knew what it just was. It was just a matter of Eddie not wanting people to know about us, and that was all right. I understood. He'd had a rough time, and me and him out in public would only make it worse. I wondered what my father would have thought of Eddie and me. If all went well, I'd be able to find out.

"Think we can fit in a quick bite before curfew?"

Eddie was quiet for some time then said, "Fuck it, why not?"

"Your dad working a case or is he cracking heads on the Night Crew?"

"Case."

"Good."

"Harry's?"

"Harry's."

We hung up without another word. No more "I'm sorry" or "I love you." If things were different, I wouldn't even go to dinner with him. There was no reason to drag out the pain. Except, now there was. Maybe after I met with Mel, I'd go down a path that would let me see Eddie again. Maybe something I did would have changed, and maybe—among other things—we would be good again.

I picked up my last envelope of money and stuffed it into my waistband. Mel would expect the money, but she wouldn't expect me to cash out. She'd always known it was coming, just not when. I'd given her and the cause seventy-five percent of my high school life. It was time for her to deliver on her promise.

I listened at my bedroom door, but I couldn't hear my Uncle J.J. He'd either be out drinking with his friends, hoping to make it home before curfew, or he'd be passed out drunk in his bedroom. He wasn't my real uncle, just a guardian for the last few years. After Dad got picked up for dealing at the marketplace downtown, the state sent me here.

I pulled open my door, snuck down the hall, and saw Uncle J.J.'s car keys on the side table near the front door—definitely passed out drunk in his bed. I grabbed them and walked outside. Not two seconds out the door, I was hit with the reminder of what this place had become.

A police squad car cruised down the street past each townhouse with its spotlight spraying white against stucco and brick. The car stopped when the light hit me in the chest. I smiled and waved, but that just made the officer get out of the car. He was a big man who looked too tired to be doing this type of work. It wasn't yet curfew, but he was on Night Crew, so he was getting ready. He had the backpack strapped on, the two-pronged volt gun at his hip, and an entire line of plastic handcuffs hanging off his belt.

He crossed the sidewalk and stopped at the base of the steps in front of Uncle J.J.'s house. "Officer," I said, looking down.

"Name?"

"Tyler Meng."

"This your house?"

"No, sir, I'm just a kid. I can't buy a house."

"Funny. Do I need to ask you for I.D.?"

I shook my head. "It's not past curfew is it? I thought I had some time to go for a quick walk."

"Where you heading?"

"Just down the block, maybe circle it a couple of times, then I'm coming right back here."

"If I see you out after curfew, no breaks. You're going in. Understand?"

"Yes, sir."

If you were picked up after curfew, you'd be held. Didn't matter if you committed a crime beyond that or not. If you were under 14, you'd be held for five days with an all-inclusive psychological evaluation. Between the ages of 15-20, you'd be held for two days and "monitored." Anyone picked up after 9pm and over the age of 20 was held overnight.

The officer grabbed his shoulder mic and spoke into it. "Bravo-34, show me on patrol, Cumberson Heights." He turned and climbed back into his squad car.

I waited for him to turn down the block before walking to Uncle J.J.'s Honda Civic. I knew there were other officers on just about every corner. That's what made the night drops so exciting. Mel wouldn't allow any of her runners to bring cash back during the day.

I lowered myself into the tiny Civic and fired up the engine. If Mel got picked up, it would be different. It wouldn't be a simple curfew violation. She was the one they wanted, but she wasn't the only one out there. I'd heard other cities had similar new laws and curfews in place. And they surely had people just like Mel, otherwise those laws and curfews wouldn't exist.

The promise of starting over, of doing things again but better, was more than most governments could handle. It was more than Eddie could handle. More than I thought I could handle when I first heard of it. But now, it's all I wanted.

A chance to start over. With my father.

It was a three-minute drive to Harry's. I pulled into the parking spot just to the left of a huge saguaro cactus with a fake needle hanging from one of its many arms. Protest art, but I wasn't sure what it was protesting. Could have been the drug, but I liked to believe people were more inclined to protest the government's crackdown on our chance to explore. The way I saw it, Jump gave everyone an out. Fuck something up, go see what else could have been. No harm in knowing what used to be unknown, what used to be impossible.

I got out of the Civic and walked into Harry's, careful to keep the envelope of money in my waistband. I wouldn't be going home after this, and I couldn't risk it being left behind or stolen. That money, along with my past service, was a ticket to something more powerful than what the general public had access to. Jump was a roll of the dice. What I'd be getting was pure control.

Eddie sat in a booth toward the back of the diner. He had a soda and was looking at a poster on the wall. I slid into the booth across from him and read the words on the poster:

You only get one life.

Only, the "f" was crossed out.

One lie.

"I know they're talking about the government, but neither side is right, you know?" Eddie said.

I looked across at Eddie, his eyes sagging, mouth turned down. It made me want to lean across the table and kiss him until he smiled, but I knew that wouldn't work.

"There really aren't sides," I said. "There is belief and a lack thereof."

"Tyler."

"I know, I know. None of that talk."

"That's how we got here."

"I just wanted to go to Winter Formal with you."

"And I wanted to go with you."

A waitress came and asked if I wanted anything, but my stomach felt wobbly like a top about to stop spinning and I wasn't sure I'd keep anything down. I told her I'd just have a glass of water, and waited for her to leave before continuing. "But you said no, and here we are."

"Is this how we're going to spend the last few minutes before curfew?"

I shook my head. I just needed to see Eddie, here and in this current life, one more time. "No, let's talk about something else."

"What're your plans for the weekend?" he asked.

The question hit me in the chest like a fastball. I couldn't breathe for a moment, and I thought about backing out. I didn't need to cash in. I could drop the money tonight and keep on living this life.

No, I couldn't.

"Nothing," I said.

"Tyler, don't be mad, please."

"I'm not. I'm just…sad."

"I can't let myself be sucked into…" Eddie waved his hand above the table, indicating me. "This."

"This?"

"Your beliefs. I can't wake up one morning after letting you in and find out you're gone."

"But I wouldn't be gone."

"Tyler, there's a new suicide every thirty minutes in our town alone. You'd be gone just like them."

Over and over, I had tried to explain it to Eddie, but he didn't get it. Jump didn't take your life, it gave you another shot. It wasn't some arbitrary mix of chemicals. It was carefully engineered to tap into the human consciousness. Mel had experienced ten different life paths before landing on this one. All of them ran parallel to each other. We're present in all of them but unaware alternate life paths exist.

"If it were as simple as just dying, being gone, normal suicide, why would there be so many people doing it? Why would people pay money to do it?"

I was raising my voice, and I didn't want to. But I'd been down this road with him. I'd tried to convince people of the possible, but I couldn't do it the way Mel did. She could tell it in a way that you had no choice but to believe.

"This is why we have to take a break, Tyler. I'm worried about you, and I can't be part of this."

"This is something special." I wanted to tell him about it again. Maybe he'd understand this time. But I didn't.

Jump allowed you to leave one life path behind and move to another one. Any decision you made in your life fractured from that moment, and created numerous new life paths based on potential outcomes from the differing decisions you might have made. Jump exposed those paths. But for most people, you don't get to choose what path—what decision—you moved to.

"I can't do this," Eddie said.

"You sound like your dad."

"Fuck you. My dad likes you, wants us to be happy."

"Sure, but he's one of them."

"Them? The people trying to save dumbasses like you from killing yourself? And what about your dad, Tyler? Where's he? Don't talk about my father, don't blame him for something you're causing."

I sighed, looked at the table. Eddie was right, but he was also proving out why I needed to do what I was doing. Eddie's father was on the outside, doing what he thought was right while my dad was living in a box.

"I—"

"Just stop," Eddie said.

This was not how the night was supposed to go. I checked my phone. Fifteen minutes until curfew.

I stood and looked down at Eddie. He was afraid. I could see it in his eyes, and I got it. I'd be afraid too if I didn't understand. But I'd wake up able to re-live a life I had fucked up. And Eddie, well, Eddie would be stuck here. I'd find him, though. In another life, I would find him, and we'd try again.

"This moment," I said, "is an example of what's possible. I'm making a decision right now, but I could have made any other choice in this moment. Those possibilities open up new paths, new lives for us to explore."

I leaned down and kissed Eddie. He leaned back at first, then he sank into it. When I pulled my lips away, I looked at him. I smiled. "I love you," I said.

"I want to say it," he said. "I really do, but I can't until you're past this."

"I understand."

I could feel Eddie's eyes on me as I left Harry's. I crossed the parking lot and got into the Civic. I had just a couple minutes to get the car back and disappear into the shadows.

*

57

The trick to avoiding the Night Crew was to stay deep in the desert or between buildings. I preferred the desert, even if it took me longer to get to where I was going. And where I was going always changed.

Mel couldn't keep herself in one place. Her videos, often broadcast on the dark web or stored on thumb drives, could be tracked if she spent too much time tethered to one spot. She'd been up and down the Midwest before heading south. She'd spent longer than normal in our town when she found it because it was a good operations base for her message and for the distribution of Jump. A border town with easy access to more product when needed. Mexico didn't care about Jump. Production wasn't illegal there, so all anyone had to do was get it across the border to us.

I used my phone to light a path through the wash, dodging cacti and scorpions I couldn't see. Mel was set up in the old bus depot. The station had closed down before I was born. Cops checked it every now and then, which is why Mel was hidden deep in the electrical room of the depot. Underground, muffled by the pops and whirs of electricity still feeding to the long-dead depot.

When I neared the depot, I crouched behind a palo verde. There were two squad cars parked in weed-choked parking lot. As I thought about how to get around the police, I slipped into memories of my father.

He was in prison because of me. I'd seen the people he was dealing to. They went from businessmen to junkies to gangsters over time. I was worried I'd come home and find him with a bullet through his head. So I did what I assumed any twelve-year-old would do. I called the police and asked for help.

Instead of help, they arrested my father. That decision, that moment, it had to change. My father had met my mother in Mexico and she gave birth here in Arizona. But she went back. I never knew her, never would. He was all I had.

I pushed away from the palo verde and moved east in the open desert as far away from the parking lot as I could get before I attempted to cross the street and enter the depot. I waited near the sidewalk in front of the street separating the desert from the depot, and I watched the cops. They were talking, each occasionally swiveling their head to search for curfew violators.

It used to be the government was only worried about the kids taking Jump. Curfew used to only apply to minors, but our "suicide" rate soared past the national average. Most border towns had the same problem since we were closer to the drug with a wider variety of users. So, to combat that, curfew was applied to everyone. If you weren't working, you had to be at home. Off the streets.

When the officers each took a sip of their respective cups of coffee, I bolted across the street. I made it to the east end of the depot and pressed myself against the concrete wall near the old entryway. The door to the main station entrance was boarded up, but I pulled on the plywood until there was a gap large enough for me to press myself through. It was dark inside, so I used my phone to find the hall that led to the access panel. The access panel was supposed to be for just that, access. But if you crawl-walked past the old equipment no longer being serviced, you'd arrive at another panel. I headed for that other panel.

This was only the second time I'd met Mel at this location. I had met her at countless other locations, though. The process was always the same. Covert. At night. Don't get caught.

To help fund the spread of knowledge, Jump couldn't be free. People paid a thousand dollars for it. The news anchors all laughed when they learned this and reported it during the evening broadcasts for a week straight.

"Paying to kill yourself?" they said with smirks. "Story at 10."

But that's the way it was. If you wanted to make the jump, you had to pay. For Mel—and presumably others out there—spreading knowledge of how Jump worked, of her other life path experiences, took money. And I'd been helping her get that money over the last three years.

I'd deal Jump after school. I'd be given an address on a piece of paper, I'd pick up the beautifully designed box containing a syringe full of Jump, and I'd deliver it. I'd collect the payment then deliver it to Mel.

I wasn't the only one, of course. A lot of kids at school did it. We never talked about it, never acknowledged each other. Eddie didn't even know what I had been doing. It was a means to an end.

An altered strain of Jump. That's what I'd get for my service.

I pushed open the second access panel and dropped down into the electrical room. There was light toward the back of the room beyond a generator. I walked past two kids with guns and showed them the envelope full of money. They nodded as they let me pass. I knew them, they knew me, but they still would have shot me dead if I was there without a reason.

When I arrived at the open space beyond the generator I saw her. Mel was sitting behind a folding table, working at a laptop. She looked up when I stepped in.

"Tyler, it's good to see you."

"You, too." I handed Mel the envelope and she removed the cash.

"My bracelet is off."

She looked up, scrunched her face. "What?"

"After three years, I can finally do it. I can use the stuff you promised."

She leaned back in her chair and smiled. "Have a seat."

I sat in the folding chair across from her and laid my hands in my lap. I'd waited for this moment from the day she told me about the altered strain. I'd dreamed of controlling the moment. Instead of some arbitrary decision point in my life, I could dictate what was important to me.

"You understand that doing this will take you to a path based on the moment you choose, but you still won't know the situation. Does that make sense?"

"It does," I said. "And I know exactly what moment I'm going to choose."

"I'm sure you do." Mel turned and pulled a box from the fire safe behind her. It wasn't quite like the ones I'd been delivering. Instead of the wooden case, it was made of smooth steel. An oak tree was etched into the lid with branches shooting out in every direction.

Each branch had smaller branches. An endless number of paths to choose from.

I reached out to touch it, but she slid the box away. She motioned to the two kids with guns near the generator. "You two, come over here and watch. Good work is always rewarded."

They came and stood behind me as Mel opened the box. Inside, the case was lined with black felt. A syringe sat in the middle. It looked the same as the ones I dealt, but I knew it was different. I could feel it. The energy pulsed and thumped my eardrums like bass from a song I never wanted to end.

"While you're depressing the plunger, you must be thinking of the moment. No second chances on this, Tyler."

"I understand."

She slid the box across the table. "I'm sorry to be losing you but happy for your journey. Wherever you land, I hope you'll get the opportunity to spread the word like I've been doing."

"I will," I said, and meant it. Whatever happened, people needed to know what was possible. They needed to be allowed to break free from the pain and suffering of mistakes.

I ran my finger along the syringe, lifted it from the box. As I held it in front of me, I thought about my father. I'd visited him once a month when he first went in. Then it was once every other month. Now, rarely. I tied a rubber band around my bicep like Mel had showed us. Pumped my fingers into a fist a few times. A fake junky going through the motions while I thought about the man who'd served real junkies.

I thought about the moment I called the police on my father, the moment I got him locked up for good. And I shoved the needle into the vein snaking its way across the bend of my arm. I let the needle rest there for a moment, and then I pressed down on the plunger.

As soon as the Jump left the syringe and entered my bloodstream, I felt it. It kicked me in the stomach and pressed me against the chair. And then I was on the ground shaking, then convulsing, then puking.

I saw Mel watching me as I spun on the floor. Then I saw the two kids from school. Then I saw nothing.

*

When I woke up, I felt groggy and sick. But I also wished I could hop up and down and dance in front of Eddie and every other person who didn't believe. The government and all their measures taken to curb suicides that were not actually suicides.

I was lying on my side on something metal and hard. I rolled to my back and saw a concrete ceiling. I laid there and remembered my old life. It was the only fair thing to do. In my past life path, people would be sad. But that was abstract now. I was here and everything around me was the only reality I needed. I rolled to my other side and looked out at this new life.

And all I saw were the metal bars of a prison cell.

I stood up and looked at the metal bed I had been sleeping on. I found a metal toilet bolted to the wall. I rushed to the bars and asked for a guard. When the guard came to the cell, I saw the lettering on his uniform: PCDC.

Pima County Detention Center.

"Why am I here?" I asked.

He laughed. "Why are any of us here, kid?"

"No, I don't remember why I'm in here. Tell me, please."

"I don't have a file on you, crazy. I just know you're here. You and your old man. The guys and I have a pool going, see how many of you end up in here. I've got my money on just the two of you, but some of the other guys think you've got a mother out there that may land in the lady jail someday. I'm a softie, though. Think two's enough for a family."

"My dad's in here?"

"Oh yeah, two blocks over."

"But why?"

The guard laughed then walked away. I stood there alone, thinking. I'd get out. This was a mistake. I thought about what could have landed me in there. After a minute, my eyes flickered and my vision went white. Then my head throbbed and I stumbled back to the metal bench.

Like a movie I couldn't control, thoughts flooded me. No, not thoughts. Memories.

I chose not to call the police about my dad that day when I was twelve. I chose to stay close to him, to help him by being there. But being there turned into something more. It turned into work. It turned into dealing. Not dealing Jump, dealing heroin and cocaine, splitting profits with my father. The memories continued, forcing themselves into the folds of my brain like a parasite. We were picked up when I was still a sophomore.

I'd been in prison for two years. No idea how much time I had left to serve. No idea how I could get out.

And I didn't have any Jump to help me escape to another lifepath.

SCARS

She touches the bubbled, rough skin below her right eye.

A rock, kicked up from the back tire of one of the 4x4s the boys drive after school.

She lays her arm on the table and rotates it so her forearm is facing up. Long, pink lines. Raised skin.

I thought I could juggle swords. Not swords, really. Kitchen knives. Like I was in a circus.

She turns in her chair, lifts the back of her shirt above the waist. She can't see it. Can't really feel it. But she knows it's there.

No, not a belt. Well, it was a belt of sorts. I tripped in the garage and managed to land right on top of dad's belt sander. And it had been left on.

She shakes her head.

My father? He always told me I shouldn't have been so beautiful. Shouldn't have been so much like my mom.

Her finger hurts when it rains, but not right now. Not as she lifts it just above the table to show the angle at which it bends to the left.

Car door.

She listens then pulls her hair back from her face, away from the skin just below her ear. She bunches her hair behind her head in a ponytail, careful not to touch the purple bruise along her jaw.

No, I couldn't say that. My dad's not like that. He's just tired of remembering my mom.

BROADWAY SUMMER

Siobhan hit him with her ring hand, open-palmed.

"What the fuck?" he yelled.

There were times when she had to step back, think about why she did what she did. This wasn't one of those times. "You said you were getting a bottle of Captain Morgan, not a stack of fucking lotto tickets."

Before he could say anything else, she hit him again, closed-fist, cubic zirconia aimed at the bridge of his nose. Matthew—or Matty P, if you believed the name on the CD he tried to sell on the sidewalk outside the CVS—covered his face. He yelled. Then he backhanded Siobhan into the headrest of the driver's seat.

"We still have two bottles back at my place," he said, wiping away the blood on his nose. "Calm the fuck down."

Siobhan pulled the rearview mirror down at an angle, looked at the blood trickling from her nose. As the blood reached the top of her lips, she imagined it giving her color—something she could never quite pull off with lipstick. She shoved the mirror back in place, and started her old Ford Escort.

They drove back to Matthew's apartment, bleeding and silent.

He had a bottom floor unit in an old pay-by-the-hour motel three blocks from campus. The motel had been shut down for a few years now, and after the university realized they couldn't turn it into off-campus housing, the city of Tempe let it go. Matthew rented his unit from a Pakistani man who Siobhan once thought wanted to fuck her. Turned out, he thought she could sell him heroin.

Matthew didn't wait for Siobhan to get out of the car. He went into the apartment as Siobhan lit a cigarette and leaned against the side of her Ford. From the parking lot, she could see the stadium lights and "A Mountain."

Joey Preston had taken her on a hike up that hill—it could hardly live up to being called a mountain. This had been senior year when she thought she'd be on Broadway in four years and Joey thought he'd be playing at the base of that hill for the Arizona State Sun Devils. He had proposed to her there, and she laughed at him. Fucking laughed like she was sitting front row at the comedy club downtown.

Siobhan stubbed out the cigarette beneath her sneaker and walked into Matthew's apartment. "Aren't you going to pour me a glass?"

Matthew flopped himself on the futon Siobhan had been using as a bed for the last three months—since they "moved in together." He looked up at her and snorted. She turned away when she saw split skin on the bridge of his nose, that weird mix of bruise and blood.

Siobhan looked back at him and said, "Please?"

"I can't get my nose to stop bleeding," Matthew said. "Lucky you didn't break it."

"Shut up," she said, walking across the apartment into the kitchen. "You hit me too."

"In self-defense."

"Who would the police believe?"

"You fucking kidding me? The police? First of all, fuck you. Second, they'd haul us both in. You want that shit? Another mark to add to your dancing resumé."

Siobhan poured half a glass of Captain Morgan, spun the lid off the two liter of Coke, and filled the rest of the glass. "It's not dance, shithead. It's theatre."

Matthew laughed and turned on the television. Siobhan watched him staring at the TV and wished she could print off a list of credits from her undergraduate program, show him what she'd done, prove to him how hard she'd worked. But he knew. He'd done the same thing. You put in the work, and good things are supposed to follow.

She poured him a glass of straight rum, sat next to him on the futon, and handed it to him. "You think you'll ever get on one of those game shows?"

He took a sip, looked at her, looked back at the TV. "Fuck, no. That's why I'm playing the lotto, baby."

"That's your big break, huh?"

"Well, at least I know when my shit ain't going to work out. My demo's going nowhere, and I need cash."

"What's that mean? My plans aren't going to work out, and I just don't know it? Is that what you're saying?"

Matthew threw back the rest of his rum. "Girl, you're 25. You ever make it to Broadway, it's going to be in the audience."

She shoved him, he shoved her back, then they both turned toward the television. Siobhan watched the pixelated rush of color. It would come in clear for a few seconds at a time then chop itself in half, then thirds, then just be sound. Every time Siobhan or Matthew stood to adjust the antenna mounted near the window, the damn thing would start working again, so they just let it be.

"What would it have been like?"

Matthew looked at her. "What?"

"If either of us had made it? You to LA, me to New York."

"Thought you said you'd come with me to LA if my demo took off."

"I thought you just said your demo wasn't going anywhere."

He shrugged and turned back to the TV.

"I'm talking about just that first step," Siobhan said. "I'm always thinking about the big picture. Making it. But what about just making that first step. How did we not pull that off?"

Matthew laughed. "Because we got stuck in Phoenix, pretending we were living through a super hot Hollywood summer."

"Phoenix—the Los Angeles of the desert."

Siobhan finished her drink and went to the kitchen to pour another. She stood behind the counter, drinking, watching Matthew. He'd been the right guy at the right time when they met in class. And he was the wrong guy at the wrong time when she received her latest rejection from a theatre program in New York—this one from NYU.

That had been three years ago, before they spent all their money on meth and booze. Before the distractions of classes faded into academic probation and disqualification. Before she was waiting tables at the Applebee's down the road and Matty P was begging people to give him five bucks for his demo.

She sipped on her rum and Coke as she walked back into the living room. "Let's do something."

Matthew didn't look up. "I need to watch the numbers."

"We'll be back before the stupid ping pong balls are pulled."

He looked at her, smiled. "There are things we could do here."

"Fuck off." Siobhan went to the door, turned around, then said, "Can't we just be normal people for a night? People who don't drink alone in front of the fucking television."

Matthew looked at her, wiped the drying blood on his nose. "You wanted the Captain Morgan."

She opened the door, glass of rum and Coke still in hand, and went out into the warm night. She stood beneath the yellow parking lot lights and drank. She couldn't see the stars through the glare, so she walked out to the sidewalk, into the darkness, and looked up. Stars danced across the black sky, spun until they were a whirlpool of light. Siobhan realized they weren't spinning. She was.

Just as she lost her balance and fell, Matthew caught her.

"This what normal people do?" he asked, smiling.

"No, they walk. They talk. They have dinner." She handed Matthew her glass and he finished off the rum and Coke. He set the glass down on the curb and took her hand. They walked past the Tempe P.D. satellite station, past the squat adobe homes with broken windows—the ones that would have been mansions when they were first built—past the group of homeless men and women the city hadn't yet forced out.

Matthew hummed a tune—something from his CD. Siobhan sang and danced in her mind, all the way back to when she was eight years old. Her mother had taken her to her first recital, and Siobhan had tripped on stage. On the way home, her mother looked into the back seat and said, "Honey, maybe you should take up something a little simpler. Like writing or drawing."

That's what had drawn her to Matthew. When she told him she was getting her undergraduate degree in theatre studies, he'd told her it was amazing.

"You're brave and talented and beautiful," he'd said.

And so was he. He didn't have reality television to propel him into a music career. He didn't even have access to a studio. But he made music. And that's why they were perfect together.

But then the local theatre auditions fell flat. Matthew's father told him to get a real job, and Siobhan's parents told her they wouldn't keep paying for her to "party."

When the memories pulled and tore at her like an itch so deep beneath the skin she'd never be able to scratch it, Siobhan chose distraction. Something to keep her mind off the past and the future.

"Let's stop here," Siobhan said, pointing at The Shanty, a shitty little bar on the last street before they got into the nicer part of town.

"I thought—"

"Let's just stop."

He shrugged and they went inside. The Shanty was dark, had two pool tables in the back, and a long bar full of college kids too poor to drink at the more expensive places close to the university. Siobhan took a stool, but there wasn't another one for Matthew.

"Guess I'm standing," he said.

"Such a gentleman."

Siobhan looked at the bottles along the back of the wall. Nothing fancy—Jim Beam and Evan Williams, Captain Morgan and Malibu. But she ordered a Bud Light. She'd been forced to share half her tips with the hostess after her last shift, and after Matthew bought those lottery tickets instead of booze, she couldn't rely on him to buy her drinks.

She listened, not to Matthew explaining to the bartender how he'd busted his nose in a pickup basketball game while ordering his whiskey neat, but to the absence of noise. She remembered the cheers and dancing and laughter in the bars near the university—the ones she'd go to when she thought she had a chance.

No, she still had a chance. Even if Matthew thought it was time to give it all up. Even if he had already given up.

"I can still make it," Siobhan said.

Matthew nodded but didn't say anything. He sipped his whiskey and watched the single television mounted above the bar. The local sports network had a replay of the Sun Devils' last loss. Siobhan couldn't figure out why people wanted to keep reliving defeat.

She took a swig of her beer. That's exactly what she was doing. While the world moved on, found new ways to get to where they needed to go, Siobhan had tried the same thing over and over. Scanning the papers, circling any promotion for open auditions, hoping this one would be the one. Didn't matter that she wasn't being trained anymore. She'd relied on that "fuck you" she wanted to wave in her parents' faces when she made it. But she hadn't done a damn thing besides relive her failures.

Maybe she'd try another undergraduate program, or maybe she'd start auditioning in Tucson.

"Fuck Tucson," she said.

"What?" Matthew leaned closed, eyes still on the TV.

"Nothing," Siobhan said, watching her beer sweat on the bar, getting warm, getting old.

A few people cleared out and Matthew, tired of standing at the bar next to Siobhan, grabbed a stool and dragged it next to her. He ordered a third whiskey and winked at her, eyes bloodshot and drooping.

"What?" she said.

"We're frauds."

"No we're not."

"Maybe we should have been bankers or grocery store clerks or fucking writers." He took two big drinks from his whiskey and laughed, spraying saliva and alcohol across the bar.

"Come on, man," the bartender said.

Siobhan looked at Matthew's glossy eyes. Writers. Bankers. Yes, the grocery store would be a wonderful place to go to die. She remembered her high school's performance of Our Town. She played Emily wonderfully. That's what they said. It was a true performance, it was who Emily was. Her growth. Her marriage. Her early death.

Maybe that's what Siobhan's life was, an early death. The fire had been lit early, burned too bright with the slightest bit of praise. Then, she ran out of fuel. And now, though she hadn't realized it, she was on her deathbed.

Matthew finished his whiskey and tried to order another. "No fucking way," the bartender said.

"One more, man. That's it."

The bartender shook his head. "Pay up."

Matthew cursed under his breath and paid while Siobhan tried to count the hours left in her life. In Our Town, Emily died giving birth, but Siobhan's story wouldn't be so beautiful. She hadn't given birth to anything—not a degree, not a career, not a life.

"See, frauds."

She looked up at Matthew hovering over her. "What?"

"We're frauds. If we were normal people, we wouldn't get cut off after," he turned toward the bartender and raised his voice, "three fucking drinks."

"You're a fraud," Siobhan said. "I'm not done."

"Sure you're not. I'll see you on the stage at the next show I catch, huh?"

"Fuck you," she said, standing.

Matthew grabbed her arm. "We need to stop pretending we're something else."

"I'm not."

"You're nothing."

Siobhan hit him in the same spot she'd struck earlier. The bridge of Matthew's nose split and blood spilled down his face.

"Bitch," he yelled, grabbing his face.

Siobhan hit him again and tried to turn toward the door, but he shoved her. She fell to the ground but got up quick, ready to hit Matthew again. The bartender jumped to the other side of the bar, cordless phone in one hand, his other pressed against Matthew's chest. "Go," he said to her.

And she did. She left The Shanty, walked back down the street toward the apartment. But she stopped and sat on the curb. She pulled her knees to her chest and closed her eyes. She imagined a life outside the desert. Imagined New York City or even Los Angeles. Places where people cared about culture more than they cared about horses and ranches and rattlesnakes.

She opened her eyes when she heard footsteps rushing toward her. She looked and saw Matthew running down the sidewalk.

"Come on," he yelled, racing past her.

Siobhan saw the bartender giving a half-assed chase. She hauled herself off the curb and ran, following Matthew all the way back to his place.

When she got there, the door was open and she heard Matthew laughing inside. She stepped in, closed the door, locked it. She sat down next to him and looked at his nose. The blood was running into his mouth. But he laughed.

"That was real," he said.

"But definitely not normal," she said, laughing.

He laid on the couch, flipped on the TV, watched as the news started. Siobhan went to the kitchen and made him another drink. She came back and sat next to him as he drank it lying down.

"There are examples," Siobhan said.

"Of what?" Matthew asked, slurring his words and drinking his rum.

"People who started late, got their break when they shouldn't have."

"Sure." His eyes fluttered, closed. But he still sipped on the rum.

"There were actors who switched careers, made it late. It can happen."

"Mmhm," he said.

Siobhan sat back on the couch, watched the news without watching it. She didn't look over as the glass of rum toppled from Matthew's hand, landed on the carpet, and spilled everywhere. She didn't listen as Matthew began to snore. All she did was repeat over and over in her head that she would make it.

She didn't know how long she'd been sitting there staring at nothing, but she noticed when the lottery number drawing began.

Siobhan looked at Matthew then looked at the table in front of them. The tickets were spread across the table like playing cards. Six tickets because, it's all about odds, baby. That's what Matthew would say. She picked them up and held them in her lap. All she needed was a chance.

As the little ping pong balls bounced around the hopper and were pulled out one at a time, Siobhan shifted through the tickets. The woman on the screen wore an awful pink blazer with a painted yellow desert sunset green-screened behind her. It made her look like a cactus bloom bouncing around the screen.

Siobhan closed her eyes, looked at the tickets. So far, a six, a nine, and a twenty had been drawn. One ticket matched each number so far, but Siobhan continued to look at the other tickets. As if the numbers would shift, give her those better odds again. With three more numbers to be pulled, she needed all the help she could get.

The pink cactus bloom woman showed her teeth, flipped her hair. Pulled a twelve. Match. Pulled an eight, another match.

The lights of Broadway. The playbills with her name on it. The applause at the end of a perfect performance. She saw it all. Didn't matter where she was or what her history was. If there was one thing more important than talent, it was money. She let herself believe she had that money, had a famous mentor helping her prepare for her big audition.

Siobhan felt those ping pong balls in the hopper move to her chest, beat against her rib cage. She didn't want to see it, so she turned her head and listened to the giggly voice from the television.

Eighteen.

Siobhan turned back to the screen to make sure she'd heard right. Looked at the ticket to make sure she'd seen right.

They all matched. Every number. She stood up, let the other tickets fall back to the table, and held the winner close to her chest.

She had no idea what the jackpot was, so she watched for another minute. She thought she heard it, but it couldn't be. Then she saw the number on the screen. Ten million. Ten fucking million dollars.

Siobhan took a breath. Matthew bought the ticket. She could wake him, split the jackpot. But he wouldn't do that. It was his money. Except he didn't know. He just knew that he bought a stack of tickets.

She went to the kitchen, grabbed her keys off the counter, then stopped. She put the keys down, held the ticket in one hand, then grabbed the rum with another. She took a shot and put the bottle back on the counter. Siobhan grabbed her keys and went to the door. She opened it as quietly as she could and closed it without a sound.

She looked at the ticket one more time after she climbed into the Ford Escort. She smiled as she started the car, planning her long drive to New York City. Then she left with the jackpot.

THE SLAMMER

"You know they call him The Slammer now, right?" The girl asked the question with hesitation, as if she were looking over her shoulder and expecting to see The Slammer there. She was kneeling on the white-hot cement sidewalk. The sun climbing, her classmates playing. The boy was across from her, bouncing on his toes.

"Yeah, duh," he said. "They've been calling him that for a while. Let's play."

The boy had a tube. In that tube were caps. His favorites were the commercialized faces of television characters hawking a product. Leonardo selling chocolate milk or Sonic the Hedgehog telling kids that McDonald's fries were the best.

The girl wanted to talk about The Slammer. He'd been at the school all along, but it seemed to her like he was new—a transfer student, maybe—after he earned the nickname. "He hits the pile so hard that you have to crawl around all over the place just to find the Pogs."

"Yep."

The girl had a tube of her own, capped off. Not ready to release upon the world a magical collection of everything from Hello Kitty to Ghostbusters. Her caps, the ones without any dents or tattered edges, were not for play. She used her brother's set when she was playing. But she always used her slammer. Her slammer was blue, a dog with its tongue hanging out imprinted on one side. A paw print on the other.

"He uses that one silver slammer."

"Who?"

"The Slammer does." She said it, brows furrowed, as if the boy wasn't listening. "His slammer doesn't have a picture. Does yours?"

"All of them do," the boys said. "Are we playing?"

"The Slammer's doesn't."

"I played his sister once." The boy took a stack of Pogs from his tube, checked his Casio wristwatch.

"Really?" the girl asked. "She played?"

"It's why he plays. She taught him how to play. Now, he doesn't even keep the ones he wins."

"But you've seen how hard he throws the slammer?" The girl stood and looked out across the sun-washed playground. "Like he's trying to throw it straight to China."

The boy looked at his watch again. "Recess is almost over. We playing?"

"One time, when I played him, he threw the slammer so hard it bounced off the stack and hit me in the forehead. He didn't take the ones he won, though."

"Did you take the ones you won?"

"Well, duh," she said. "I gave them to my brother. I was playing with his Pogs."

The boy looked at the girl, shook his head. "You shouldn't have. Those were his sister's."

"Who's?"

"The Slammer's sister."

"So?"

The boy laughed. "I wish you would play me. You're so dumb, I'd probably take all your Pogs."

The girl stood and shoved her tube of precious Pogs under her arm. "Shut up. I'm not dumb."

"You took those Pogs from his sister."

"No, I won them from him."

The boy turned now and walked past the girl. On his way past he said, "Have you seen his sister lately?"

The girl turned, watched the boy walking away. "No, why?"

"Why do you think he throws the slammer so hard?"

The boy disappeared into the classroom, and the girl wished she hadn't taken The Slammer's sister's Pogs.

COYOTE

She crossed northwest of Sonoyta, just south of Ajo, in the Organ Pipe National Monument. Carli Echeverria was on the first leg of what would be a two-leg journey. After she made this drop, she'd make another run further north. To Tucson or Phoenix or Gila Bend.

She looked over her shoulder, the rear window of the Nissan pick-up pressed right up against her seat. The truck's bed was just long enough for three small dog kennels. The first kennel, nearest the tailgate, held two dogs. The two kennels behind it were stuffed with blankets.

Behind those blankets were people.

Carli tried to fit five or six people in the two kennels with each load. Today, she had seven thanks to a couple of children making the run.

After she picked the group up at a gas station in Sonoyta, they walked west toward the crossing point. The Nissan was tucked behind a collection of organ pipe that rose ten feet into the blue, desert sky. In her experience, getting to America was the easy part. Once there, she needed help. She relied on an old C.B. radio in the Nissan's cab. If a lookout spotted Border Patrol, Carli would know. And she would adjust.

They were on Highway 86 heading toward Three Points when Carli passed the spotter tower. Two weeks ago, the radio crackled just before she came across that same spotter tower. The lookout told her to hook a left and head further north down the dirt roads. A temporary checkpoint had been set up that day, and if not for the lookout, Carli would have been sent to secondary inspection. She would have been forced to sit while a dog sniffed up and down her truck, and they would have found her load.

Not today. The highway was empty, quiet.

Carli flipped down the Nissan's visor and let a pair of aviator-style sunglasses fall into her hand. She put them on and pulled her white cowboy hat lower across her forehead. She watched the heat dance in waves across the recently paved highway.

She wasn't supposed to be there. Not in that moment. Not in that life. She was supposed to be better than her mother. And maybe she was. She was out here doing something while her mother was locked up. Or in the back bedroom of a one-room trailer with her legs in the air. If Carli's mother was out, there was no telling where she would be. Could be back home in eastern California. Maybe Mexico. She didn't want to think about it. Didn't care.

She shouldn't complain. The money was more than she'd ever make anywhere else. Even if she had gone to school—and goddamn, it seemed they gave scholarships away to Mexican girls just for checking the box that said "Latino"— she would never make the kind of money she was making now. Over time, she'd learned to convince herself what she did was just an adventure in the desert as she helped people to freedom.

But it was hard to maintain that fantasy anytime she came across the charred body of a crosser who had succumbed to the heat.

Most coyotes didn't last more than a year. They needed quick money and got out when they had it. Or they stuck around too long and got caught. Carli, though, had made more runs in her time than every other runner in the crew combined. Yet, she could feel the weight of it lately. The ghost of the person she didn't want to be was riding shotgun, and it was begging for the steering wheel.

She watched the saguaros and barrel cactus slip past her on either side. She thought about the people she helped cross. They didn't all make it, but everyone paid. Getting to America was never free.

Carli kicked her boots together, letting her left heel run just above her right ankle. A reminder of the .22 tucked just inside her boot.

She'd only had to use it once. Couple months back, a group tried to run on her as soon as they crossed into Arizona. It wasn't the first time and it wouldn't be the last. Carli rounded up this particular group, but one of the men tried to run again. She didn't have a choice.

After she put a round in his left triceps, the rest of the group fell in line. She caught hell when she dropped him at the stash house with a piece of his own shirt tied around the wound. She didn't get paid at all on that run, which was bullshit. She'd delivered every one of them. Even if that big dumb fuck had a hole in his arm, he was alive.

It was shit like that. Made Carli wonder if she could keep this up. You see so many things before your brain decides it can't see them anymore. The real world was out there, waiting if she wanted it.

She tapped the steering wheel and laughed, imagining what her responses might be now to job interview questions in the real world.

"Tell us about a time you overcame a challenge."

"Well, I had to shoot a man just to make sure I got a job done."

"So, you're committed to your work then?"

The smile faded as the thought slipped away. It was only going to get worse. There was a time when she thought she could control her life. Now, with every new job, every fight she had just to get paid, every horny old man trying to fuck little girls, it became clearer that this life controlled her.

She tilted the rearview mirror toward her face. A few strands of black hair escaped the hat and dangled near her eyebrow. She was surprised by the wrinkles around her eyes.

Carli shoved the mirror away and watched hints of a town spring up along the highway. A gas station. A small shopping plaza. Oases in the desert. The town barely existed.

She turned down a dirt road and watched the dog kennels bounce as the truck fought the dips and divots. Eroded sand, baked under triple-digit heat, was hardly an excuse for a road. She passed a house every mile or so. Mobile homes parked on acres of land. Custom homes, built decades ago. Constant reminders that Three Points was somewhere people chose to live.

She parked the Nissan in a clear lot south of what was meant to be a guest house. The main house was thirty yards to the north with an attached garage and a paved driveway—despite the nearest paved road being five or six miles back.

She got everyone out of the dog kennels and led them to the guest house. She knew it'd be empty. A conveyor belt of order governed her life. One group cycled from the main house to a car or truck for the final run north. The group in the guest house moved to the main house to make room for the newbies.

Carli unlocked the back door and led them in. The windows were barred. The front and back doors had multiple deadbolts. In the living room, she waited.

In the beginning, she laughed at the reactions. She didn't understand what they had expected when they agreed to let someone smuggle them into a foreign country. She used to feel powerful as these people saw their new home. Trash in every corner. Piss stains on the floors and walls. Shit swept into a single corner of the house. Now, she looked away.

After leaving the group in the guest house, locking them in as she left, Carli backed the Nissan up the driveway toward the main house. The conveyor belt never stopped.

The main house wasn't much better than the guest house. The drywall had holes throughout—either from immigrants trying to punch their way out or an enforcer who just didn't have the patience to watch another woman or child cry. As best Carli could tell, the benefit of being moved into the main house was the bucket. Like the guest house, there wasn't any running water, but there was a five-gallon bucket in the living room.

Leopoldo Ruiz ran the house. He was also second-in-command of the crew that worked with the cartel to smuggle people across the border. Carli considered herself more of an independent contractor, but she guessed Leo was technically her boss.

She walked past the empty living room. Leo didn't keep anyone in there anymore. Too much shit to clean up. Too big a space. He stuffed them all in the back two spare bedrooms. Carli made her way down the hall past the kitchen, toward the bedrooms.

When she found him in one of the rooms, Leo was running his fingers through a teenage girl's hair. The girl, like the rest of those in the room, was clad in just her underwear. A sweat-stained pair of panties and a tattered bra.

The girl closed her eyes and turned her head as Leo whispered in her ear. Everyone else in the room pretended not to notice.

"Having fun?" Carli asked, standing in the doorway.

Leo jerked his head away from the girl and looked at Carli. "*Sí, siempre.*"

"*Esa es tu novia?*" Carli said.

Leo pushed the girl away, who huddled near the rest of the group. "Why you got to fuck up my mojo, Carli?" He stood and patted Carli on the shoulder as he passed into the hallway.

Carli followed him into the living room. "They ready?"

"Ready as they will be," Leo said. "As if my hospitality wasn't good enough for them." He spit on the floor, a mixture of tobacco and saliva joining the other stains on the bare concrete.

"Send them out then."

*

Carli locked two dog kennels in the bed of the Nissan. She slid the third one—the one with the dogs—back toward the tailgate, concealing her load as much as possible. The dogs barked until Carli slammed her fist down on top of the kennel. She looked in the two kennels full of people and did a quick count.

Missing one.

"Fucking Leo," she muttered, looking back at the main house.

Her boots clicked against the cracked cement driveway on her way back into the house. She scanned the property one more time before entering. No tracks nearby. No movement. Just empty, brown, dusty desert. The neighbors weren't much of a problem because of the distance, but she didn't want some kids on four-wheelers romping through here and catching a glimpse of something they shouldn't see.

Inside the house, Carli yelled for Leo. He didn't respond. She shook her head as she went down the hallway. He wasn't in either of the two spare bedrooms, so she stepped into the master. Leo was straddling the teenage girl. Her bra was flipped up near her throat, and Leo was staring at her breasts. He touched her stomach. Then her cheek. The girl squirmed, but she didn't scream.

"Jesus Christ, Leo," Carli said. "I need a full load."

Leo laughed. "You don't need shit."

"She paid, right?"

"Sure. Her family wired the money a couple days ago." Leo squeezed the girl's cheeks until she cried out, kissed her on the lips. "But fucking look at her. *Qué bonita.*"

Carli's face grew hot. Her hands started to shake. "I need her. I've got to make the final drop."

Leo shook his head. "You're not getting it. This one's worth more. More than what her family already paid. The way I see it, I've got two options that'll make us some extra cash. We rent her out—you know these old white fucks around here will pay for her. Or, we ransom her. Tell her family she's going to be fucked six ways from Sunday if they don't pay extra. A beauty tax. What d'ya think?"

She watched Leo licking the girl's ear and wondered how she'd been able to put up with this shit for so long. It wasn't just Leo, and it wasn't just the girl. Carli was a professional. She wanted things done right and on time. Leo fucking this girl was not part of the plan.

Leo winked and told Carli to get the fuck out, but Carli stood in the doorway. She should leave. She should make her run north, but her face was getting hotter. If Leo made more money off the girl, it didn't mean more in Carli's pocket. Just Leo's. In fact, her cut at the final drop would be less. She'd let shit like that slide too often.

She felt the sweat on her forehead. Her hands trembled noticeably now. Turn around, she thought. Go. But she didn't.

"Leo, I'm serious. I need the girl for this run."

Leo stood and squared himself in front of Carli. "You don't fucking tell me what you need, bitch. I tell you what I need. I need you to get the fuck out of here unless you want this to turn into a three-way."

Carli thought about hitting him, but she stepped toward the girl instead. Leo shoved her in the chest, and Carli stumbled then tripped and fell to the floor. She was up in a second. The heat from her face moved to her eyes, and everything went white for a second. She backed up a step, bent over, pulled the .22 from her ankle holster, and pointed it at Leo. He took a step back, but Carli was already firing.

The first bullet hit Leo in the shoulder and he fell near the girl. The second sailed high. Leo tried to slide backward away from Carli. He held both hands in front of his face. Carli stepped across the room, but she felt like she wasn't doing it. She felt like she was watching herself. Like she was hovering outside her body, unable to stop what was about to happen.

Carli pointed the .22 at Leo's forehead and pulled the trigger one more time.

She blinked away the white heat as the gunshots echoed in her ears. When the ringing subsided, she holstered her gun and turned. The girl had folded herself into a ball in the corner. Carli looked back at Leo.

"Fuck," she said then punched the floor.

She could run, but the girl was there. Terrified. "*Esta bien,*" Carli said. "*Estás seguro.*"

She helped the girl to her feet and asked her name.

"Mitra," the girl replied.

Carli pointed at the girl's upturned bra. "*Pon eso de nuevo.*"

They left the room together. The girl didn't say anything, but she stood close to Carli. The run was over. Carli couldn't take them all to the final drop. Word would get out. Someone would be waiting for her if she went north.

"*Dónde está la ropa?*" Carli asked.

Mitra pointed toward a bathroom set off from the living room. Carli followed her and found the group's clothes thrown in a bathtub that was black with mold. She helped Mitra get dressed and gather the clothes then pointed her out the front door.

In the driveway, Carli hesitated when she got to the dog kennels. She could leave them there. Maybe that'd soften the blow. No, she thought. No amount of goodwill now would change the end game.

She unlatched the dog kennels with people inside. Five immigrants climbed out, confused. Two women and three men. Carli helped them down from the truck. Mitra passed out the clothing, and they all dressed.

"*No puedo tomar,*" Carli said.

Carli remembered the group in the guest house. She ran to the guest house and threw open each lock. She led the group she had just dropped off back out of the house.

"*Todos ustedes tienen que ir por su cuenta.*"

No one moved.

"*Sal de aquí,*" she yelled.

After another moment of silent looks between each other, the group started to move. They began a trek toward the open desert, away from the main road. Carli grabbed Mitra by the elbow and held her back.

"*Quédate conmig,*" Carli said.

There was money in the stash house but not enough. Carli didn't think there would ever be enough money to keep her alive after what she did. She lifted her hat, pushed her hair back, and closed her eyes. Behind closed lids, she saw Leo bleeding on the floor. She opened her eyes and pushed Mitra toward the main house again. Money bought a lot of things. If it couldn't buy her life, it could extend it.

Back inside the house, Carli led Mitra to the middle of the living room and told her to stay put. She went to the refrigerator and pulled open the door. The light inside had probably been out for years. There was a box of baking soda on the top shelf. Other than that, the entire thing was seemingly empty. Except the bottom drawer. It was covered with black electrical tape. As if keeping someone from seeing into the drawer was enough to keep the person from opening it. Nice, Leo, Carli thought.

Carli pulled the drawer open and found three large envelopes. She ripped them open one at a time and lined her pockets. She stuffed as much cash into her pants as she could, but there was still a lot left over.

She called over her shoulder for Mitra. She told the girl she wouldn't hurt her if she helped. When Mitra came over, Carli began handing over stacks of cash. She pointed to the pockets of Mitra's jeans, and the girl began stuffing. When all the money had been emptied from the envelopes, Carli walked Mitra back out front. When they returned to the driveway outside the house, the rest of the group had vanished. If they were nearby, they had become invisible. Silent. Carli smiled. She could disappear, too. For a while, at least.

She couldn't run, so she thought about the next best thing. A safe place to hide.

She looked at the Nissan. She'd have to leave it here. Too many people in her crew and in the cartel knew it. She might have to steal a car. Or maybe she'd let her hair fall down her back, let her hips sway a little more, and walk along the highway with her thumb out. Whatever she did, she'd make it, and Mitra was coming with. Leo's beauty tax plan wasn't half-bad, after all.

Carli pulled her hat low, watching the sun sink behind Kitt Peak. She took Mitra by the arm and they walked. She was going to California. Going home.

CREOSOTE

Reyna felt the clay beneath her palms, hard and cracked, hot. She heard the hawks overhead. She felt the sun baking her skin, peeling it back and exposing muscle and bone. She felt the land taking her, but she held on. She reached out and felt for the bush.

Hands wrapped around it, Reyna remembered what her father had said. He'd called it *el arbusto del agua*—the water bush. He told her creosote was made from rain. She wanted to pull it from the ground, hold that creosote near her nose so she'd never forget the smell of those dusty summer storms back home. Hold it to her eyes so she could always see the lightning cutting through the sky. Press it to her ear to forever hear the crack of thunder.

And she wanted to put it to her lips so she might taste another drop of water, so she might continue on if even just for a few more minutes.

They'd left her hours ago. Or days ago. Reyna wasn't sure. The first water jug, left out for people like her had been cut, water long since evaporated back into a sky that would never need it as much as she did. The second jug had been cut as well. By the time her group reached the third and found it cut, Reyna fell. To her knees at first, then to her stomach, arms to her sides, face pressed into the dirt.

Reyna asked them to wait, but they said, *"La migra nos atrapará si esperamos."* She asked them to help her, but they said, *"Sólo pagamos para ayudarnos a nosotros mismos."*

She asked them for water, but no one had any. So they left her. They marched on through the desert, hoping to find a jug of water that hadn't been cut by people who didn't want people like her there.

And now, all Reyna could do was free her mind as the sun reached down from the sky and scratched at the back of her neck, at her face, at her arms and legs.

All she could do was reach for that creosote bush and remember what her father had said.

MIRACLE MILE

There's still some neon left. Every night, a few old motels flash pinks and yellows and greens, but the rest of the strip is dark. There was a time when Miracle Mile was alive with beautiful lights, restaurants, temptations for road-weary motorists. I let the blinds fall back in front of my window.

All that's left now are the temptations.

I turn back toward the open room, and she's staring at me. Claire stands by the front door of our studio apartment, shifting her weight from one foot to the other. "This isn't the end, Howie. You know that, right?"

I nod and she starts to twirl her hair with the finger she broke the night I met her.

That was shortly after I had grown tired of using overnights at the Pima County lockup to keep me from slipping. I had been looking for something new. But they don't make support groups for what I got— at least none I've found. So, I figured I'd try the next best thing. The closest Narcotics Anonymous meeting was a couple miles from my studio, in the auxiliary hall at Saint Elizabeth Ann Seton's. She was on the steps when I arrived late.

"You alright?" I asked her, although I wasn't sure she was awake. Her face was turned toward the concrete steps, her back rising and falling as if she were sleeping. Then she puked, turned the steps a light yellow with bile.

When she rolled onto her back and fought for fresh air, I saw her finger. "I fucked it up," she said, holding it out toward me. "When I fell."

She told me she must've been late to the meeting. When I asked her why she thought that, she said, "Because I'm already high."

We didn't go in that night. We decided a trip to the diner off the interstate made more sense, and by the time we finished our food, we'd formed a plan. We didn't need meetings.

I'm not sure why I told her what I told her while we ate hard pancakes and drank cold coffee, but because I did, she's here. Or, she was here. Now, she's on her way out.

"You remember what this place looked like when I moved in?" she asks.

I look around the studio. Milk crates hold up a plywood tabletop, two lumpy mattresses lie against the wall closest the kitchen, and a television Claire found on the curb in front of the apartments is propped up on what I think used to be a bookshelf. The television never worked, but it made us feel like real people.

I shake my head and smile. "I remember the stains you made me cover up, and that a sleeping bag wasn't a good place to sleep."

"So you agree, I made life better for you." She laughs, turns her head toward the door, then turns back to me. "I've got to go."

I nod because there's nothing else I can do. I could beg, but it's her father we're talking about. Her daughters. For the first time in three years, she's got a shot. That her old man took care of the girls this long means he can't be all that bad, even if he did leave her to puke in the gutters and figure shit out on her own.

She moves across the living room, her hair falling behind her. Shinier than when we met, fuller. Her skin is clear, scabs healed long ago. Claire leans in, kisses me on the cheek, hugs me, then holds my cheeks in both hands.

"I love you, Howie."

"I love you, too."

She smiles and walks back across the room. We bought her new clothes last week. She's wearing the jeans I picked—the ones she said she hated. They would have fallen off when we first met.

At the door, she taps her fingers against the faded wood. She doesn't turn. "Don't slip."

"You either."

Now, she spins around. "I'm serious. I'm here, and I want you to call me when you need me."

I smile and tell her I will. I don't need to make the same promises and suggestions to her. She'll be all right.

She blows me a kiss and walks out the door.

In the wake of her exit, I see a question mark. I know the question, so I suppose I don't need to see the words that go along with it. It's floating right in front of me but too far away to touch. It must be like the floaters my mom used to see before the start of a migraine. Before she'd pass out in her bedroom.

The first time my mother mentioned them, I was six. That also happened to be the first time Dave came into my room in the middle of the night.

I stand and look at the two lawn chairs. I fold one up and place it against the wall next to the front door. I walk to the window and look out again. In my head, she's down there, staring up, waving at me. But in reality, there's just the road and a dirt lot across the street with a few weeds fighting through the dry earth.

The interstate marks the horizon, cars rushing by, not daring to detour down the strip. Not that they should. I wouldn't want them to.

You don't make friends with anyone but the voices in your head here.

I push away from the window and look at her mattress. I pick it up and drag it on top of mine, then I fall into the cushion of my new bed. It had been months since she last slipped, but I expect to smell the vinegar sweat-soaked sheets I'd grown used to when she was still trying to prove she could quit. Instead, I smell her perfume, and close my eyes.

That last time—when I made the mistake of leaving her alone too long and she came home covered in piss and missing her purse—she crawled on top of me when I tried to put her to bed. She pressed both hands under the waistband of my basketball shorts. I pulled her hands out and slipped out from under her. She passed out that night before she could be embarrassed or angry.

The next day, I told her there was a time when I would have tried. Or let her try. She asked me why I didn't, and I told her about the neighbor woman who lived near my mother's old place when I was a kid. The one who smiled and winked at me every time I passed her house. The one who invited me inside on a hot afternoon.

Claire asked why I would have gone inside the neighbor's house. "Because I was sixteen and needed to know," I'd told her.

We made a deal after Claire's last slip. She would never go out without telling me where she was going. I wouldn't go more than twelve hours without seeing her. And most important, we'd talk every night. And for her end of the deal, she'd be there. Just be there. She broke that part of the deal, but I'm glad she did. It's better for her.

I fall asleep, but the first gunshot of the night wakes me around eleven. I stand by the window, waiting for a round to shatter the glass. None come. No more shots, no lucky bullets carving their way through my walls to get rid of the question mark for good.

There's a liquor store on the corner. Alcohol had been out of the question because of Claire, but maybe I'll get a six-pack and think. I start for the door then remember where thinking gets me. So, I sit in my lawn chair and stare at the blank television screen.

But the thoughts have already come. I think of boys I've never met. I see them there on the screen. The first one I see is about nine. He's playing ball on a field near where I grew up. He's not real. But he's there, throwing the baseball on my broken television. I close my eyes and beg Claire to come back.

When I open my eyes again, I'm no longer sitting. I'm pacing the living room. I stand over the phone Claire bought us three months ago. She thought it'd be good to have a way to call for help if we needed it, but I think she knew she was getting better. Closing in on a new life. I think she knew I'd need the phone more than her.

I'll call her.

No, it's been just a few hours. That's ridiculous.

I do fifty-seven push-ups before collapsing face-down on the dirty carpet. Back when trips to jail were my form of therapy, I had gotten up to a hundred and sixteen straight. I'm pissed at myself that I can't keep going, but then I'm not. I wish I didn't have to do a single push-up again in my life.

I lie on my bed, using Claire's scent to keep me occupied. I hear voices calling back and forth across the street below my apartment. Young voices. I stand and look out the window. The neon from the Old Wrangler Motel flashes and pops across the black puddle near the middle of the road. I can't find the kids who are calling out, but I see a woman walking in high heels and a short skirt.

Besides needing a cheap place to stay, that had been the reason I moved here. Before I met Claire, I thought I could buy my way out of my head. The first girl cost two-hundred and fifty dollars and she laughed when I couldn't get hard.

The shrieking siren of a police cruiser sends the woman scurrying for the nearest alley, but the cop isn't after her. I watch the cruiser's lights flash past on its way to something more violent. I walk to the front door, lean my back against it, and slide to the floor. My life isn't worth thinking about, so I think about Claire's.

When she was eighteen, Claire was arrested for the first time. She told me she spent years thanking God for that arrest because she met her dealer in jail. "Such an easy path from pain to forgetting with a dealer you could trust," she'd said with a snort.

Claire's daughters don't know their fathers. She told me she was probably high when each of them was conceived.

I think it made Claire feel better that I hadn't known my own father. I'm not sure why. The logic of me says that her girls need to know their father or they'll be fucked up just like I am. But that's not what Claire thinks.

"The truth is, you're stronger than every fucking one of us. The junkies, dealers, the whores down there walking the Mile. You're better than us all, Howie."

"How's that?"

"You haven't given in. You're fighting like hell, man. No one fights like that."

She never could understand the fact that I hadn't fought hard enough. By the time I was ten, I could have stopped him, but Dave kept coming. Once a week, twice a week. Sometimes, he wouldn't show up for days on end and I'd find myself crying into my pillow wishing he'd open my door and sneak in after my mother fell asleep.

I slam my fist into the floor and shake my head. I can start over and forget everything, but no, I can't. I just end up remembering the Sunday after my high school graduation.

I know it was a Sunday because I was walking past the church I'd been baptized in—the one that used old saguaro ribs to form a cross on the outside wall. Everyone was spilling into the parking lot, shaking hands and basking in the glow of God's love. The boy broke free from his family and ran into the middle of the parking lot, did a flying karate kick, and landed like he was a superhero—one fist to the pavement, head up, eyes strong. I didn't go toward him, didn't keep looking when the boy's father ushered him to their car. But I saw him all day in my mind.

I cut myself that night.

There are a million things you can do to take your mind off something, but as soon as you get to one million and one, that's when you're fucked. I roll onto my side, pull my knees to my chest, and fall asleep.

*

I made it three days before finding old distractions. I punched a homeless man in front of the police station, spent the night in jail. I broke into PJ's Liquor on the last corner before people escape Miracle Mile for the interstate. Spent a couple nights in jail.

Now, I'm back in my apartment, staring out the window as the sun rises over the Catalinas. The blown-out bulbs and shattered signs lining the strip reflect long shadows that do little to calm my mind. The shadows are pointing across the empty lots, beyond the damaged arms of saguaros unfortunate enough to grow around here. They point me somewhere I can't go.

I smell Claire's perfume despite the spoiled jug of milk I left on the counter before my last stint in lockup. I see strands of her hair sway and shimmer in the morning light. I'll grab them, put them together. I'll build a new Claire.

She hasn't called. She has the girls, her life. But I haven't called either.

I have the six-year-old version of myself clawing at my brain. He's sitting in my head, on the couch his mother used to hold him on. I have the ten-year-old version of myself soaking my shoulder with tears.

The carpet beneath the windowsill is cold despite the morning heat coming off the single-pane glass. I sit with my legs folded under me. The room seems brighter than when Claire was here. It's probably just because the blinds have been open more. Claire preferred hiding us away from the world, lest its temptation suck us back in.

After Claire moved in, a temp agency found her a job downtown filing paperwork for an ambulance chaser. She took the bus to work, ate leftovers at her desk, then came straight home. Like a horse with blinders. The only time she let herself see was when she was home, with me.

One night, when she was pounding on my chest, begging me to let her downstairs and down to the corner for a quick score, I suggested we buy a board game. We bought Monopoly, and we played until the sun came up.

I stand and walk to the closet by the front door. Monopoly rests on the top shelf. I pull it down and hold it in both hands. The game is heavy in my hands. I could open it, play it alone. Pretend. But I always knew there'd be a time when I had to admit what I was.

I throw the game across the room. The box splits open, game pieces bouncing across the carpet. When I leave the apartment, I bring the curious six-year-old version and the desperate ten-year-old version of myself along.

I walk past the cemetery at the far-east end of the strip. The funeral home sits on the opposite corner of an old taco shop, boarded up and tagged with spray-painted words. I step down into the wash cutting between the cemetery and the road. My shoes sink into the soft dirt that feels out of place among the hard clay and rock everywhere else.

I step around a stray jumping cactus and kick my way through the rusted cans and broken glass being swallowed by sand. I beg for a flash flood to sweep me away. Three feet below the road above, I picture myself carried through the wash, downstream, to wherever these things spill out. Maybe it would take me all the way to the Santa Cruz River.

Before the wash ends in a metal-framed tunnel, I emerge at street-level. The tire shop at this intersection—where I've never seen a single tire replaced—is boarded up. Yet, I know there are people inside. It's the place Claire pointed to when I asked her where she scored after her final slip. She told me it had been a Mexican restaurant back in the fifties. Now, it's a hole in the earth.

I'm going home.

But I end up walking past my apartment building. I know where I'm going, and it's not home. I try to think about other things. The gas station a couple blocks up where I found out the last car I had couldn't be fixed. The motel I saw lit up by bullets one night two years ago. The Sonoran hot dog stand that'll open in a couple hours.

I shake my pocket and know I have enough change to treat myself. But I'm not going to be on the strip in a couple hours when the stand opens.

I turn and walk down Flowing Wells, past the police station. Just three miles from the elementary school. Miracle Mile is behind me, crying for me to come back. The wraiths of what the strip could have been tiptoe alongside my parallel life. The one where I broke free of this.

"You never break free," Claire told me a few months ago when I asked her what she'd do when she was done with addiction. "It's not a fix and forget it kind of thing. It lives inside you. It's like a cancer that you can always beat back into remission if you try hard enough."

She might be right. But the way I see it, this life is nothing more than a stretched rubber band. You can only pull on it so many times before it snaps.

It's funny thinking back on what pacifies. All Claire did was listen to me. If that's all it took to keep my mind in check, I wouldn't be half a mile from the school right now.

To be fair, I didn't do much more for her. I hugged her when she asked, I listened to her when she didn't ask, and I played board games until the sun came up.

Thinking about it, thinking about her, steals my breath. I suck in, but the air doesn't reach my lungs. She's going to land right back where she was. I try to catch my breath but it won't work, and I cough and slap at my chest. I let her walk back into the world, unprepared, into a cycle of remission bound to break.

When I stop walking, the air comes back to me. I cough and try to turn around, but I keep moving forward instead. The school is right there. Quiet. The kids won't break for lunch for another couple hours, which means they'll be coming out for recess right about—

The first line of children rushes from the main brick building across the street. I wave a slowing city bus by as I sit on the bench at the bus stop. The playground is bordered by barrel cactuses placed every five feet around the perimeter. And a chain-link fence, of course.

After each burst of children running in groups escapes through the door and onto the playground, a boy—maybe a fourth grader— walks alone, head down. He doesn't go to the playground. He walks around the side of the building and sits on the bench nearest a payphone standing on the sidewalk in the parking lot. The farthest spot he can get to without leaving the confines of the school yard.

My right leg bounces in place, and I watch him. The boy's eyes search the ground in front of him. He lays his hands in his lap. The other kids laugh and scream and jump from the monkey bars. This boy watches a quail half-fly half-run across the parking lot.

I watch the bench he's sitting on melt into the same one I'm sitting on. The world pulls us together, and we're no longer on Flowing Wells Avenue in front of the school, but we're in a '57 Bel Air with the top down on Miracle Mile. The sun has fallen behind us and the neon is alive. Every hotel, bar, and restaurant sings with life. The hookers and junkies are gone. Replaced by couples walking hand-in-hand, high school kids trying to score booze. The boy and I just drive, comfortable.

I'm sweating. Everyone's sweating, but I'm drenched. It's not yet eighty degrees, no excuse for this. Claire's voice is knocking on my eardrums, trying to get through.

"My daddy told me there are some things you just got to figure out on your own." She said that to me the first time she told me about her father. Then she said, "I call bullshit on that one. Nobody figures out jack on their own."

I scratch my forearm just above the scars until her voice goes away. Then, the boy looks up. He looks at me looking at him, but he doesn't turn away. I don't know what comes next, not sure what to do. So, I stand up. I break eye contact first, looking to the street just in front of the school. I shove my hands in my pockets, jingle the change with my left hand. When I look up, the boy continues looking at me.

Curious eyes.

Claire's voice tells me it's all one big choice, then I walk into the street. I wait for a cab to pass by, then I make it to the sidewalk in front of the school. The boy's eyes have never left mine. They are begging me to get my closure as I near the fence.

But I turn up the sidewalk, and I walk into the school's parking lot. I keep watching him as I reach the payphone, and he watches me. I lift the receiver, praying for a dial tone, and I get one. I drop the change in and dial Claire's number. When she answers, the boy is no longer looking at me.

CHASE

They're going to ask why she did it. They're going to wonder why it happened with two kids strapped into car seats in the back. They're going to call her a monster, take her babies away. They're going to prove out everything he ever said about her.

But only if they catch her.

Leilah had always joked with the kids anytime she got to drive the old Malibu. "Want me to go fast?"

Her youngest would smile and grip the straps of her car seat. Her oldest would chant, "Do it, do it," as he kicked the back of her seat.

But she saw them in the rearview mirror now, and they knew it wasn't a game. Maybe it was the wailing sirens. Maybe it was the helicopter above them. Or maybe it was that turn three blocks back where she clipped a moving truck and lost the passenger side mirror.

Leilah pulled hard on the gearshift, put the Malibu into second while jamming on the clutch and brake. She cranked the wheel right and saw the interstate.

Get to it. Head south. Then she'd lose them among the weekend traffic heading to Mexico. She wouldn't be able to cross, of course. They'd stop her in that log jam of people and cars. But, if she was lucky, she'd slip between clumps of traffic, dart off an exit heading east through Santa Cruz County, watch the helicopter fall back as she closed in on Cochise County and the Fort Huachuca army base.

It would work. Had to work.

"It's okay," Leilah said to the mirror more than her children. Her daughter stared out the window. Her son cried.

No, she wasn't a bad mother for this. Not even her babies could convince her of that. They'd understand one day. If she had to tell them.

Thomas was the one who'd wrapped his hands around her neck one too many times. Those hands and that whiskey. He'd said the water—one finger for every two of the good stuff—kept him level. "It ain't a problem, baby. Not when I mix it up like this."

Bullshit.

What he meant was it wasn't a problem when she didn't say shit about it. When she let him push her up against the wall and breathe into her ear. Breathe that fire across her neck. It wasn't a problem as long as she didn't mind the bruises.

Highway Patrol joined in as soon as she climbed the ramp onto the interstate. No spike strips, though. Not yet. They fell in behind her with the city police and the sheriff's deputies right on their tail.

It'd always been Leilah's fault. She married him. She knew him. She let him drink, let him put his hands on her.

"Mommy," her son said, his eyes wet and his hands balled up in his lap.

"It's ok," Leilah said. "It's ok."

No, it wasn't her fucking fault. That was what he wanted her to believe. That's what he'd always said, tried to convince her of. This—the car, the police, the southbound trip to nowhere—this was all Thomas.

She looked in the rearview one more time, caught her daughter's eye, smiled. Earlier, when Thomas didn't stop at one glass or two or three, and when he got angry at the way Leilah looked at him, he reached up into one of the high cabinets in the kitchen and came out with a gun. Small thing, dull gray. Leilah had started to say something about it—about where he'd gotten it—but she didn't have the chance before he fired a shot through their townhome wall, through their daughter's bedroom, shattering the mirror near the window.

That was it. Leilah scooped up both kids, grabbed the keys to the Malibu, buckled the kids in, and ignored Thomas. Ignored the still-hot barrel of that .38 as he pressed it to the back of her head.

"Get the fuck back inside," he'd said.

She ignored that too.

By the time she peeled out of their driveway, the police were flying down the street, but she didn't stop. Couldn't stop. She knew what happened next. She'd seen it before. Friends from high school, her cousin in Tubac. Wasn't such thing as an aggressor and a victim. Both parties would be hauled in.

She wasn't going to let them take her babies. Not even for a few hours while someone hopefully sorted things out at the police station. And they might not have ever sorted things out. She wouldn't allow it.

But now, she was driving seventy-five miles-per-hour southbound toward Mexico with no real outcome beyond losing her babies anyway. And he was probably back home, talking his way out of any trouble. Telling them she'd been the one to fire that gun. Telling them he had to wrestle it from her hands, but he wasn't able to stop her from taking his children. He'd cry and beg them to stop her, but not to hurt his babies.

His fucking babies.

Leilah pressed down on the accelerator and ignored the sounds of her daughter's cries now mixing with her son's. She ignored the sirens and the squealing brakes of other cars as their drivers realized what was happening. And she hit the I-10/I-19 interchange hoping to lose a few of the Highway Patrol cars.

She didn't.

Leilah slowed as traffic swelled. The Santa Rita Mountains rose in the distance, bouncing on the horizon, giddy for a front row seat to Leilah's escape. She remembered the canyon out there by the base of those mountains. Her father had taken her as a girl once.

"You drive around in her long enough, you'll get lost," he'd said before they finally found a spot to park and camp.

She closed her eyes only for a second, long enough to remember which exit to take. Exit 37. She could make it. Then she'd lose everyone.

Leilah reached back and touched her son's knee, but he slapped her hand away. "Stop, mommy."

Her daughter wailed.

Leilah wasn't the bad guy, she wanted to scream. She'd saved them from the bad guy. She wanted to hang her head out the window and shout it back to all those police following her. She wasn't the bad guy.

The exit was 12 kilometers away. Fucking metric signs. She tried to do the math and convert that to miles, but couldn't. Wasn't far, though. She'd make it.

She passed a convoy of vans filled with church groups, doing the Lord's work. Rescuing people who never knew they needed to be rescued.

Over the crest of a small hill, she saw the exit. But just ahead of that exit, Border Patrol had moved their temporary checkpoint from the northbound lanes to the southbound lanes. No. No, no. That didn't make sense. They didn't need to check southbound drivers.

But Leilah already knew why they'd done it. She saw the one lane to the right packed with cars. The lane to left wide open, spike strip lying from shoulder to the white-lined middle of the highway.

She looked in the rearview and saw the police cars piling up behind her. She heard the helicopter chopping at summer air. She looked back at her kids, at her babies.

Thomas was the bad guy, not her.

She kept to the left lane, pressed her foot down harder on the accelerator and closed her eyes.

LIVING IN AN ECHO

This one isn't smooth, not like the others I've visited. This one has sharp edges that slice at the wrinkles on the back of my hands. This one trips me when I think I might be walking a straight line for a change. This one builds walls that close in every time I try to escape.

I've visited other echoes before. Still do. But they all live inside this one now. Just like I do. Trapped forever with the sound of his voice.

No, not his voice. His words.

"Fuck you." And "Bitch." And "Whore."

Echoing.

Sometimes I wonder if it was the words that did it. Just the words. But that would let him free, let him have some sort of out. It wasn't the words. It was what he'd done before those words. Before I leveled his daddy's old snubnose at his chest.

Inside the echo, I have a life. I put on a face, drive to the mall, meet my friends for dinner. Inside the echo, I'm on a stage. Broadway, under the big lights. I have to be because no one understands the echo, the trap.

His words, rattling around in my head. Holding me forever unless I do something about it. But there's nothing to do. I already did it. Ended it, but didn't end him. The first echo, the one that came from the tip of that gun and curled back to my ears, that echo faded instantly. Replaced by a scream, a thump, sirens and shouts. But those all faded too. They were there, trapped inside this echo just like me.

But only for a moment. Their moment is over, but mine never will be.

THE GIRL IN THE TARP

John Campbell drew a picture thirty years ago. That picture destroyed his marriage and cost him his daughter. That picture hangs on his kitchen wall. Just above the table. Her face—made of graphite lines and charcoal shading—was innocent, clean. Nothing like it was when they found her in the desert.

He held his old nightstick loosely as he stood on the doorstep, remembering her. The girl in the tarp. She took his attention away from his wife and daughter. She destroyed him, but she was destroyed first.

By the man on the other side of the door.

John's retirement pin and new gold watch—resting back home on the table beneath the picture—were fresh with the smell of celebration. Only, the end of his career was not a celebration. It was a declaration that the girl's death would go without justice. With him out of uniform, no longer chief of police, sitting at home, she'd be just another forgotten face.

He wouldn't let that happen. That's why he was visiting Hector.

Hector Renteria didn't ask about her family. He didn't ask what they did with her body or how she'd be taken care of after the fact. He came forward with information, but he didn't act like a witness or a concerned bystander. Hector told police he wanted them to know where the tarp found at the scene could be bought. Said he had one just like it at home.

John knew it right away back then, but he was young. His gut worked, but it couldn't explain to him what it felt.

Hector was the only suspect. He inserted himself in the investigation right away. Over time, John had seen guys do the exact same thing. Every one of them was fucking guilty. And he knew Hector was guilty too. But they let him walk.

John knocked on the door. Hector wasn't expecting him, but John visited often. He wanted to make it clear he'd always be there. Watching and waiting for Hector to slip up. Official interrogations and unofficial visits in the dead of night were all John had as he continued to put the pieces together over the years. He had held out hope that something would break. Or that Hector would confess. But time was up. Hector's wife was out of town, and Hector's children were grown and living on their own. This was John's last shot.

The door opened a crack and John kicked it. Hector stumbled back, and before he could regain his balance, John swung the nightstick. Wood against flesh and bone. The skin above Hector's cheek split before he went down. John hit him again, and Hector went limp.

John ran his hand along his pistol. He could do it right there. End him. But he wanted to make Hector admit everything. He'd have to take Hector out of town for that. John was too well known around the city. He couldn't risk doing it anywhere nearby.

Despite the obsession, despite the broken marriage, despite the nights he stayed up begging God to let him forget that girl, John rose through the department. What was once an unexplained feeling in his gut—the same one he felt with Hector—became detective's intuition. From sketch artist and patrol officer to detective on up, John learned to use that intuition.

He hog-tied Hector with disposable zip-tie cuffs, opened Hector's garage, and backed the Crown Victoria in. He shut the garage and dragged Hector to the car. He popped the trunk and lifted Hector in, John's back cracking and popping with each movement.

The street was quiet. It was two in the morning, and John could hear the night. Warm air slid between the rows of tract houses. He pulled the Crown Victoria out of the garage and drove to the freeway.

It was a four-hour drive out to the dunes. East to New Mexico. He had the air conditioner on high, but John was sweating through his white button-up. The gun belt—the same one he'd worn to work every day—pulled tight around his jeans, dug into his gut. He could hear the blood rushing through his ears.

The girl wasn't even buried after she was killed. Just wrapped in that green tarp. Dumped and forgotten. Her face was gone when they found her. She'd been there for months, rotten and half-eaten by animals. John had to bring her back to life with his pencil. He had to give her a face so they could figure out who she was.

And he did. He drew her. They passed the picture around to every news organization in town. John's drawing hung in every post office within fifty miles. It was the first thing talked about during morning briefing, and it was the last thing John thought about when his head hit the pillow at night.

No one claimed her.

John thought he heard a thump from the trunk. He turned off the AC. He strained his ears, waited. Nothing. Just the road beating back against the Crown Victoria's worn tires.

He was worried he would kill Hector with the blows from the nightstick, but Hector was breathing when John dumped him in the trunk. If only he would stay unconscious until they got to the dunes.

John flipped the air back on, let his mind drift. Margaret wouldn't have left him if John had dropped the case. If John had kept up with her, helped out, she'd still be with him. More importantly, Jo would still be with him.

"This is a two-person job," Margaret's voice screamed in his head. When she left, she took Jo. John wanted to fight, but he didn't. He told himself he'd be able to see Jo. They weren't leaving town after all. But he didn't.

The pounding started a few minutes after John got gas. They had crossed the New Mexico state line and were only an hour or so away from the dunes. White Sands, New Mexico: where the girl in the tarp would finally get a name.

John tried to ignore it. He focused on the light rising up from the horizon. The sun was about to crest the mountains in the distance. That was fine. The dark was no longer his ally. He just needed the dunes and their quiet isolation.

The girl's face danced across the windshield as John fought sleep. His eyes drooped, but she kept him awake. He remembered her teeth. Even with most of her face gone, he saw the teeth and could tell they weren't quite as large as they should be. When he drew her, he focused on the mouth first. He worked his way out from there. A soft, rounded nose. Thin lips. Wide eyes. Short, blonde hair.

Margaret would beg him to forget the case. She didn't think it mattered. But they had a daughter. Of course it mattered. The girl could have just as easily been Jo. But Margaret never understood that. She couldn't understand the need to find the girl's family. To give her a name.

Jo was young enough that John could force her to the phone after Margaret took her away. They'd talk for five minutes about nothing, then it'd be done. As she grew older, Jo stopped coming to the phone, and John stopped calling. He picked the phone up hundreds of times over the years, desperate to hear Jo's voice. But he couldn't dial.

The pounding from the trunk grew louder. John kept looking back, expecting the trunk lid to fly open and Hector to jump out. They were close. He'd make it.

White Sands might attract people from all over, but it's too large a space to fill. Two hundred and seventy-five square miles of dunes. Tourists stayed close to the road and facilities. The offroaders stuck to the larger, easily accessible hills. John would take an access road he found a while back. He'd drive about ten miles deep into the dunes, then he'd cut across the soft sand as far as the Crown Victoria would take him. From there, he'd make Hector walk.

With his turn approaching, John thought about her grave. The girl in the tarp was buried in a state cemetery. No headstone. Just a marker. Just like any other unclaimed body.

Before Margaret had enough and took Jo, she caught John carrying flowers out the front door. "You bought her flowers?" she screamed. And he had. He bought her flowers because someone should have cared enough to do so.

The sun dumped buckets of light across the black tar highway. It did its best to blind John, to keep him from finding the access road. But he found it and made the turn. The road was once a paved route for park employees to run from the highway out deep into the dunes in case of emergency. Now, with the park almost entirely unmanned, the road was a dusty reminder of how easy it was to forget.

John saw a few cars at the rest stop and the facilities just off the highway before he turned down the access road, but once he made the turn, he was alone. Until he heard the pounding again and remembered Hector in the trunk.

The road ended after about ten miles. When it did, John steered the Crown Victoria into the sand and prayed it wouldn't get stuck right away. At first, the car bounced through the sand with little effort, but soon, the soft sand caught the wheels and wouldn't let go. He checked the rearview mirror and couldn't see the access road anymore. He wasn't sure how far he'd made it, but he pressed the gas pedal to the floor and hoped to make it just a little further. After another few minutes, the sand swallowed the wheels. They wouldn't even spin, let alone propel the car forward or backward.

John grabbed his nightstick and got out.

There were nights when John would stay up, unable to sleep, thinking about the girl. More recently, thinking about the girl and thinking about Jo. John had a family, he had Jo. Then he didn't. Someone had the girl in the tarp. He'd think about that family when he couldn't sleep. They were out there, holding out hope that their missing daughter was still alive. All the while she was buried and forgotten by damn near everyone else.

He needed to know how Hector came across the girl. How he knew her. If he knew her before he did what he did.

Standing at the trunk, John watched the sun turn the sand into piles of tiny diamonds. The natural metals of the earth, caught in the morning light, lit the ground around him. He ran his finger along the butt of his pistol. It was an old .32, department-issued years ago and hopelessly out of date now.

Hector shook the entire car as he banged around inside. John tucked the nightstick under his arm, slid the gun from its holster, and unlocked the trunk. He stepped back as the trunk rose and pointed the pistol at Hector's head.

"Stop moving."

"John, what the fuck is this?"

"I'm gonna cut the ties around your feet and we're gonna walk. Walk and talk. Sound good, Hector?"

"I ain't got shit to say to you, man," Hector said. "Just take me home."

"You'll have plenty to say today."

John kept the nightstick tucked under his arm as he fished a folding knife from his pocket. He leaned in and cut the tie around Hector's feet. Dropping the knife back in his pocket, John grabbed the nightstick with his free hand.

"I told you over and over again, you need to stop fucking with me," Hector said through gritted teeth.

Hector's eyes were red, his brown hair plastered to the sides of his head, strands snaking across his forehead. John saw the gray above Hector's temples. When Hector was first brought in as a suspect, he was in his late twenties. Youth on his side. Now, he was an old man. John hoped that meant he'd be ready to talk.

"Get out," John said.

"Fuck you."

John pointed the gun between Hector's eyes. "Get the fuck out."

Hector struggled, but he sat himself up in the trunk and threw his legs over the edge. As soon as Hector slipped off the back of the car and into the warm sand, John hit him in the stomach.

"Just so you know I'm not fucking around," John said. "Let's walk."

Hector marched a few paces ahead of John. "What's the plan here, huh? You're a cop. You can't do this shit."

"You know this place is surrounded by the military?" John asked. "It's true. Military bases all around. I heard they used to fuck up, and stray missiles would come flying into the dunes. You believe that?"

Hector didn't respond. They walked until sweat coated John's back and Hector's neck shone in the sun. Hills of varying sizes surrounded them. In a valley of white heat, they finally stopped.

"Right here," John said, poking Hector in the back with the nightstick.

Hector stopped and turned around. "What now?"

John hit Hector in the knee with the nightstick and watched him topple to the ground.

"I want to be as clear as I possibly can be," John said. "I'm going to hurt you, Hector. How bad I do is up to you."

Hector settled himself on his knees and looked up. "I don't know what you want me to say. I don't know shit. Never did."

John whipped the butt of the .32 forward and cracked Hector in the forehead. Hector folded at the waist, cursing into the sand.

"How'd you find her?" John asked.

Hector straightened his back, looked John in the eyes, and said, "I didn't find her. Never saw her before your people found her."

"Goddamnit, Hector. This isn't like the other times. When I tell you this is your last chance, I fucking mean it."

"John, calm down, man. I don't know shit. I've been telling you for years."

"Tell me again then." John lifted the nightstick to his shoulder.

"It's a damn tragedy, that girl. But I didn't touch her. I never saw her in my life."

John brought the nightstick down hard on Hector's collar bone. The crack echoed across the sands. Hector fell and John kicked him in the stomach.

Between shallow breaths, Hector begged. "Stop, please. Stop."

"She was in your truck, right?" John asked. "Let's start there."

"No, man. No. She wasn't."

Hector forced himself back to his knees, but John kicked him in the face. Blood sprayed from Hector's nose, staining the white sand. He spit out a tooth and sat up.

"You're gonna die out here, Hector. Tell me something to keep that from happening."

Hector cried. "I didn't do anything, John. I swear. I swear. I didn't."

"Look me in the eye and tell me that again."

Hector looked up and before he could speak, John brought the butt of the gun down on his cheek over and over until Hector fell once more. The blood soaked the sand around Hector's head.

"You can't last much longer."

Hector spit blood, coughed, and turned his head toward John. "Fuck you."

John's hand shook as he stretched the gun out in front of him. His finger danced across the trigger, twitching. Begging. Then, he let his finger slip away.

"Just talk. This will all be over as soon as you tell me her name. Or, fuck, just tell me where you picked her up. Something."

When Hector sat upright again, John saw the swollen nose, the purple cheeks, the half-closed eyes. Hector would be knocked unconscious soon if John kept this up.

"Nothing has changed, John. I saw the news report about her. Wanted to help. That's all. I promise you, that's all it was."

Hector's voice rose with each sentence. Pleading. Convincing.

"If I kill you out here, how long before your family has a body to mourn over?" John moved the gun back and forth between Hector's head and chest. "How long before your kids can quietly walk past your closed casket and say their final goodbyes?"

"What about your family, John? You can't kill me and walk away. You wouldn't leave them behind and go to jail for this."

"I don't have a family."

After not being able to bring himself to call Jo, John tried Margaret a few years ago. He got her number from one of the police databases. He just needed to know how his daughter was doing. When he finally got ahold of Margaret, she hung up as soon as she realized it was John. He didn't call back.

"Did you find her on the side of the road? Was she a runaway?"

"I didn't do anything."

He knew it might knock Hector out, but John didn't care anymore. He swung the nightstick into the top of Hector's head. It split the skin right along the part in his hair. Hector fell forward, face down in the sand. He didn't move for a few seconds, and John worried he was dead. Then a cough. A moan.

Hector rolled to his side and got back up to his knees. The blood from the wound on his head dripped down his face.

"Fucking do it already. Kill me, John. You want to do it? Just pull the fucking trigger."

Hector cried again. His nose ran. His cuts bled. His face swelled. And John still didn't have any answers. The girl's killer was on his knees, refusing to admit anything.

John pressed the barrel of the .32 against Hector's forehead. "Do you remember how you became a suspect in the first place?"

"Because I tried to help." Hector tried to stop the tears and spoke through dry heaves. "Because my wife asked me to help."

John laughed. "Jesus Christ, Hector. We would have figured out the places you could buy that fucking tarp on our own. We weren't completely fucking stupid. You wanted to be part of it. The investigation. It gave you a thrill to tell us you had the exact same kind of tarp, didn't it?"

"I told you because I thought the killer might have bought the tarp at the same place I bought mine."

John softly tapped the nightstick on Hector's forehead. "You know, I wasn't sure what I felt when I heard you came into the station back then, but when I got a look at you, I knew it was something. I knew you were the guy."

"No," Hector cried. "I didn't do anything. I didn't kill her."

At the station, John had watched them talk to Hector. Before he was officially a suspect. When he was just a guy with some information. He sat in a rolling chair near the front desk, excited. That was it. The excitement in Hector's face.

"Everyone I talked to—press, public, cops—had faces that went long at the mention of her. You, though. I watched you give your information at the station. Eyes wide. A smile damn near creeping across your face."

"That's not true. It made me sick thinking of that little girl out there in the desert."

John hit him in the stomach with the nightstick, then hit Hector in the back when he doubled over. On his face, in the dirt, Hector took quick breaths before getting up again.

"I need you to tell me you did it. Just that much. Just admit what you did."

Hector shook his head. "You can kill me and I'll go knowing I was a good man. Didn't do a damn thing wrong."

John remembered the day detectives let Hector go. They held him for twenty-four hours. It was all they could do. John was on patrol when he got word that Hector went free. All he could see were Hector's wide, excited eyes at the station when he talked about her.

What John saw in Hector that day at the station, and what he felt every day since, was more than something clawing at his gut. It was a goddamn truth. John had never locked a guy up who wasn't guilty. He could see things in a suspect's movements. In their body language. In their eyes. John knew Hector did this. Knew he killed the girl in the tarp.

"Look around you," John said. "Is this where you thought you'd die? It'll be hot soon. Your dead skin will bake. It'll burn right off your body. When they find you, they'll need an urn. This place is a fucking crematorium. But you can avoid that, Hector. You can. Look at me. Just look. Just tell me you did it."

Hector's chest rose and fell with each uncontrollable sob. He could barely get the words out now. "I didn't—I couldn't. I love my wife. My children. Please. I didn't kill that girl."

His words were thick. They rested themselves on John's shoulders. They sunk into John's skin. Just as John felt himself believing Hector, he pointed the gun at Hector's forehead and pulled the trigger.

The body fell. Blood flooded the sand. John dropped the nightstick and stepped back. Watched. The gun shaking in his hand, John turned and tried to remember where the car was. He wanted to run. He wanted to scream, but first he had to get to the car.

Then he remembered it was stuck. He could walk back to the road. He just had to find it. John picked out the nearest hill. With each step toward it, he felt like he was sinking further into the ground. Like the sand was gripping at his ankles, trying to drag him under. He imagined the ground eating him alive. Sand filling his eyes and ears and nose. Still, he walked.

At the top of the hill, sweat soaking through his shirt, John rolled up his sleeves. The sun rose quick. It beat down. It lit him on fire. John looked all around him and saw sand. Just sand. He couldn't find the access road. He couldn't see the Crown Victoria anywhere. He wasn't sure how far he and Hector had walked. He wasn't even sure which direction they had come from anymore.

John sat at the top of the hill and looked down at Hector's body. He closed his eyes and saw her. He saw his sketch. For the first few months after she was found—after John sketched her back to life— he found himself comparing her to his own daughter. They were about the same age. They were both beautiful, blonde girls.

The sound of wind racing across particles of sand passed through John. He held his eyes shut tight. The sketch changed. He now saw a sketch of Jo. He imagined her mouth moving on paper, telling him she loved him. Then, her skin fell away. In clumps of pulp, the paper tore and Jo's face fell apart. Bone ripped through her skin. Her eyes disappeared. She was the girl in the tarp. She was the body.

John opened his eyes and let the light fill his pupils and erase the thought. He stood and unbuckled his gun belt. He let the belt drop and untucked his shirt. John tried to get his bearings once more, but it was useless. He couldn't remember where he'd come from and where he needed to go. He searched the endless sand and started to walk.

He still didn't know who she was. Still didn't know how she died. And as the shadows stepped across a sandy ocean of hills and valleys, John realized he still didn't know who killed her.

GALAXIE UNDER THE STARS

Joey had a 1963 Ford Galaxie. It was a piece of shit. But I didn't have anything except the old ten-speed my mom gave me before she split for Phoenix on my sixteenth birthday. And that didn't make for the best getaway vehicle.

"Pull the plate," Joey said while tossing a duffle bag into the backseat.

I looked around his parents' garage and wondered what they might be wondering about us. If it was my dad, he'd probably just think I was jacking it to one of the old Playboys he knew I'd found in his nightstand back when I was fifteen. But Joey's parents were different. Sitting in the living room watching re-runs of Who Wants to be a Millionaire, Joey's old man might have slipped his Miller Lite into a koozie and wondered if his kid was about to get himself killed. Joey's mother—she would've been flipping through an old Home and Garden—might have asked herself if Joey would make it to college graduation before getting arrested. After all, Joey's brother didn't even make it to high school graduation. Derek, he got himself popped at fifteen years old for running cases of hard cider out the back of Tom's, a grocery store just down the road.

"Pull the fucking plate, Mike," Joey said again, this time standing right next to me.

I grabbed the screwdriver off Joey's father's workbench and got to work. Three screws and the rear plate fell right off.

"Where's the fourth screw?" I asked.

"I don't know," he said. "Ask your sister."

I didn't have a sister, but I laughed anyway and slid the license plate into one of the drawers on the workbench. "You got the other one?"

Joey leaned into the Galaxie and pulled out a different license plate. He handed it to me and I started to ask about it, but stopped. Didn't matter where it came from. I screwed it in place and thought about the days when Joey and I didn't need to go to this much work just to steal something.

Ten years ago, Joey and I were too young to be left at the mall by ourselves. But my mother did it anyway. Thirteen with no money and no idea when Mom would be back. We didn't have much choice. We had to steal from the toy store.

Neither of us suggested it. We both just ended up there, walking down the empty aisles, lifting toys of the shelves, putting them back. Then, at the back of the store, I looked up and spotted a black dome. A security camera. "Do it on one of the other aisles," I told Joey.

"Do what?"

"Take something."

"You fucking take something."

So I did. And he did. Nothing too expensive, though. We got out of there with a couple Nerf guns shoved down our pants.

I stood back up after getting the new plate on, and asked Joey if he'd caught the Suns game.

"Fuck the Suns," he said. "Lakers, man. Lakers."

"The fucking Lakers? Since when?" I went around to the passenger side of the car and climbed in.

"We live one hundred miles from where the Suns play. Why should I care about them?"

"Because you live a hundred miles away, and because the Lakers are five hundred miles away." I popped the glovebox in the Galaxie and pulled out the .38 revolver I'd stashed there earlier in the night. I flipped open the chamber, saw it was loaded, locked the chamber back in place, and tossed the gun back into the glovebox. "And fuck the Lakers."

Joey shook his head, went around to the trunk, popped it open. I couldn't see what he was doing, but I knew he was checking the spare. He had a blow out on the highway to California six months ago. No jack stand, no tire iron, no spare tire. He sat there for hours. So now, he checked the spare tire on his piece of shit Galaxie every time he went anywhere.

Even when he was about to go rob a gas station.

Joey shut the trunk and came around to the driver's side. "Let me tell my folks we're heading out."

"Sure." I watched Joey head inside and thought about the first time his parents let me stay the night. My mother hadn't yet split, and my old man still cared enough to beat the shit out of me. That night, it'd been a fight about cigarettes. I hadn't even smoked them, just had the pack in my pocket, but Dad didn't care. Said he'd rather raise a piece of shit thief than a smoker. I bet he'd never considered I'd be both. But that night, I cut the screen on my window, slipped out into the rock and clay behind our house, barefooted. I walked the three miles to Joey's house, cutting through washes and dodging cacti. Joey's mom asked if I was alright. Joey's father grunted. But they both helped me get settled in for the night.

Joey came back out into the garage, two ski masks in his hand. "We almost fucked up."

When he slid into the driver's seat, I took one. "Where'd you even get these?"

Joey fired up the Galaxie's engine and backed out of the garage. "My brother went to Ruidoso every winter with the whole soccer team—school-sponsored trip, or some shit. He's got a shit pile of these laying around."

We hadn't talked about who was going in. I assumed Joey thought it'd be me since he was driving. I figured it'd be him because, well, because it was his goddamn idea. Back in junior high and high school, we sold the shit we stole. Worked out a hell of a lot better than keeping the junk we got tired of after a day or two. Joey made enough to buy the Galaxie. I made enough to buy weed.

I pulled the baggie of joints from my front pocket, passed one to Joey, and lit one for myself. He shook his head, but before he could actually say "no," he was lighting up.

"How much you think they keep in the register at a place like that?" Joey asked.

"A thousand at most."

"And you don't think we can get the guy to pop the safe?"

"Can you fucking read?"

"Fuck you, Mike."

"The signs outside every gas station in town make it pretty clear. The clerks can't open the safe."

Joey turned down a dirt road that led toward the main drag we'd take. There was a gas station off Fifteenth open twenty-four hours that saw almost no customers after eight at night.

"Seems kind of fucked up, you know?" Joey asked, blowing smoke out the driver's side window. "They just leave these clerks there to get their brains blown out if some robber wants the safe?"

"Why would someone blow the clerk's brains out?"

Joey stuck his arm out the window and flicked the joint into the night. I watched its cherry glide across an endless sheet of stars before disappearing into the brush.

"Think about it. Guy comes in thinking he's going to score big. Clerk says, 'No, I can't get into the safe.' Guy thinks it's bullshit, starts getting pissed. The clerk, he can't do a damn thing, and that pisses the guy off more. All of the sudden, the guy's got a gun to the clerk's head, promising to pull the trigger if he don't get the money from the safe. Clerk is crying now, still can't do shit. Guy pulls the trigger without thinking."

"What the fuck is wrong with you?"

Joey didn't say anything for a while, and I knew we were both thinking the same thing. When we hit the paved road and started the mile-long drive past old streetlights, beat-up trailer homes, and ranches that haven't seen work in decades, I popped the glovebox. Pulled the .38 into my lap.

"I'll do it," I said.

Joey shook his head. "No, I have to."

"Why?"

"My plan."

"So?"

Joey sighed. "Look, my brother's been locked up a few times now. We haven't seen him in over a year, and I don't know if he's in or out right now. So, if someone gets popped for this, who is it going to hurt less, me or you?"

"We won't get popped."

"This isn't stealing toys at the mall, Mikey."

I didn't say anything. I looked out the window. He knew I'd let him do it. He wished I would have argued more, but he knew all along I was going to stick him with the shit job. Because I'm a shit friend. I finished my joint, tossed it out the window, looked over at Joey, then handed him the gun.

"You didn't load it, did you?" he asked.

I'd forgotten Joey wanted the gun just for show. I'd loaded it a few days after we bought it downtown. But fuck it. He didn't know what might happen in there. He might need to fire off a warning shot. Might need to blow a hole in the register if the thing got stuck. There were a hundred different reasons Joey might need the bullets in that gun, but he didn't need to know they were there.

"No, it's clear."

When we made it to the gas station, there wasn't a car in sight. The two pumps outside had dim, yellow lights overhead, and the brick convenience store was lit from the inside only. Joey pulled into a spot right out front. He looked at me and nodded.

I pulled the ski mask on, and he did the same. I didn't think there'd be cameras, and even if there were, this was the type of station where they wouldn't be recording. Still, no sense in risking it.

Joey took a breath, looked at me. "Slide over as soon as I get out. Keep it running. I have no idea how long this will take."

Of course he fucking didn't. We'd stolen toys and televisions and iPhones. We'd stolen from people's apartments, their cars, their purses. Everything we stole had to be converted into money. This would be the first time we stole actual bills that we could spend right off the bat.

"Keep the gun in your hoodie pocket," I said.

Joey nodded, slid the .38 into the front pocket of his hoodie, pulled the hood over his head, and climbed out of the Galaxie. I climbed over the console and into the driver's seat as he shut the door. I'd expected him to hesitate. To stumble, then gather himself. But no. Joey was on the sidewalk out in front of the store in a second, his hand reaching for the door in two.

He walked into the gas station's convenience store as a twenty-three-year-old with twelve college credits under his belt and hopes of at least nailing down an associate's degree. But that's not who I saw enter that store. I saw my fat friend from elementary school. The kid I met on the basketball court after my head came up into his nose and blood sprayed everywhere. I saw the kid who entered junior high with his brother's shadow following him around. I saw the kid who'd said, "fuck it," and decided to live his own life. And I saw the kid who kept me from sliding down the drain when my mom went away.

They say you can't blame your choices on other people, but fuck that. I decided I could blame anyone I wanted for anything I did. Had Mom not met that realtor up north, had Dad not been such a pussy, I wouldn't be sitting here waiting for Joey to come back out with barely enough money for me to get a week's worth of weed.

He pulled the gun.

I hadn't noticed at first. But there it was, hanging from Joey's right hand. I hadn't expected him to need it. I thought he'd be able to tell the clerk he had a gun, and that'd be enough. But no, Joey had the .38 pointed at that pock-faced kid's chest. The kid behind the counter seemed pissed, not scared, but he held his hands up and backed away a couple steps.

I saw Joey yelling something, and the kid turned toward the register. There we go. Get the money, get the fuck out of there.

I looked over my shoulder, half-expecting to see Tucson PD rolling up behind me, but the road was clear. I looked out beyond the road, into the desert across the street. In the sky, the clouds slipped past the moon, and the desert shed its darkness for a moment. Infertile land that gave us just enough to survive. An offering. A chance. But it would never be enough. Nothing would ever be enough.

When I turned back, Joey was looking out the glass door, looking at me. He nodded.

No, dumb fuck. Watch the guy.

The clerk noticed Joey's distraction, seized the moment. The clerk reached beneath the counter, hit the alarm, then came back up with a shotgun in his hands.

Joey must have heard the movement, because he turned back at that moment. He saw the gun, jumped back.

And he pulled the trigger on the .38.

"Fuck, fuck, fuck," I said, pulling the shifter into the reverse, foot still on the brake.

The bullet tore through the clerk's black polo. It hit the kid in the stomach or the chest. Fuck, I couldn't tell. But it blew the clerk back against the cigarette rack. He fell to the floor, and Joey looked at the gun. Then he dropped it to the floor, looked out the window at me.

He would have been dead, I told myself. Had it not been loaded, Joey would be the one bleeding out on the dirty linoleum floor of that convenience store. But he was alive because I loaded that fucking gun. He should thank me. He would thank me when he got into the car, but Joey didn't move. He sat on the floor, his legs half folded under him.

I reached for the door handle, considered dragging him out. But there wasn't time. I didn't know how long it'd take police to get there after the alarm had been triggered. Probably a few minutes. But everything had slowed down. It could have been a few minutes already for all I knew.

I slammed my hands down on the horn. Held them there. Waited.

Joey didn't look. He closed his eyes and leaned his head back, grabbed the top of his head, right through the ski mask. But he kept it on. Kept himself hidden.

I had to go, but it was Joey. It was the only person who'd ever really given a shit about me. He helped me ask Shelly Donaldson out on a date freshman year. He'd given me one of his old man's beers when Shelly broke up with me three months later. Jesus, it was fucking Joey.

But it didn't matter.

I opened the door, swung my left foot out into the crumbling tar parking lot. As soon as my foot hit the ground, I heard the sirens. Joey heard them too—had to—but he didn't move.

Joey looked at the gun lying a few feet away. Looked at me. But he didn't try to stand. I saw the other outcomes in that moment. I saw Joey, chest blown open, lying on the floor. I saw me and Joey in that Galaxie cruising back to his house, counting the money we'd just scored. I saw the police knocking on my door three days later. I saw Joey hopping a Greyhound as I was led through lockup to my new cell.

But no. Joey wouldn't have left me. Even if I had to leave him.

Joey pulled his mask off, and I did the same. I tossed mine into the passenger seat and swung my left leg back inside the Galaxie. Joey watched me shut the door, watched me ease back out of the parking spot. He watched me peel out and watched me leave my best friend.

The freeway east to New Mexico was flashes of white painted stripes under the yellow headlights of the Galaxie. Cacti and dust and three thousand pounds of metal carrying friend away from friend. Chased by an ocean of stars that wouldn't let up, telling me that they'd always be there.

Reminding me.

FAMILY PHOTOS

There was a story on the front of every single one of them. As soon as their lock-screen lit up, the story came to life. Wives, husbands, brothers, sisters, daughters, sons. Sometimes, the story was sad in its obscurity. Say, an icon or a flag or a number. Sometimes, it was happy—or something representative of happiness, like a smiley face. But most of them held stories of family, and those were the phones I was interested in.

It didn't matter where I was, there were always stories to take. The coffee shop where I used to go to order a coffee and a kids-size hot chocolate. The park where my daughter used to run up and slip down the slide no matter how many times I told her to stop. The baseball stadium where I once taught my daughter she could do anything she wanted.

Everyone left their phones out, everywhere. So I stole their photos.

It's a simple move, really. I unlock the phone, open the photos app, click the photo and choose to email it. I email it to myself, because who cares? They aren't going digging through the sent folder on their email. If I come across a phone that's locked with a passcode, I move on. There are enough to choose from.

Normally, I take the photos of children, happy and smiling for the camera. Sometimes, I take the ones of the whole family. The dog and cat pictures are just for quick smiles.

I never think about taking one that looks like her, though.

Until today.

I was scrolling through my photos, taken all over the world by people I'd never met. But they were people I felt I knew. I smiled until my chest hurt. Until my heart beat too hard against my ribs. When that happened, I knew it was time.

I picked up my keys, and I drove out to the closest fast food joint I could find. Ordered a burger and fries. While I waited for my food, I looked at the unattended tables. Tables where people let their phones sit for anyone to take. Or for anyone to look at.

The first phone I picked up—a blue Samsung—had a lock screen picture that made my knees buckle. I grabbed the table and slid into the booth. I held the phone in my hands, looking at the picture of the little girl with the black curls. The little girl that was my little girl.

Only, she wasn't.

I wanted to keep staring. I unlocked the phone, found the picture, and hovered my thumb over it. Ready to steal it. But I couldn't. Instead, I pulled out my phone and scrolled through the photos again.

I escaped into my world, not this world. I was gone, if only for a moment.

I wanted my fake family. No, I needed them. I found a boy and a girl—my son and daughter, I told myself until I couldn't believe it anymore. I swiped on, found a man that would have been my husband's age. I looked at him for a long time, but my other hand was already reaching for the blue Samsung, lifting it before my eyes, showing me my daughter, only not.

I placed both phones down on the table and cried until the person who owned the blue Samsung came back and asked what I was doing with his phone.

I told him I was looking at my daughter, then I walked away, leaving my fake family behind.

ENDLESS WHITE SEA

I'm driving that car, and Bre's sitting next to me laughing. I can't remember what she is laughing at, but I know I'm laughing with her. I love her more than I thought possible. I feel it like a pulse beating stronger than that of my own heart. It's warm and happy. It makes me feel invincible. And that's why I'm in that car.

It's an old Celica, white with aftermarket rims. We're rumbling along the empty roads leading from Flagstaff toward forest-covered mountains.

She thinks it'll be funny to roll down the window even though it's twenty-two degrees outside. The snow blows past us in dusty white ribbons as she opens us up to the cold. Her brown hair kicks up around her.

She's seventeen and I just turned eighteen. We're four months away from graduating. That's when they all said it would change. After high school, they said, we'd fall apart. But I can't see that as I'm shivering, laughing, and watching her hair float around her like a glowing aura.

The road is dark. We haven't seen a car for miles. Still, I'm looking for something. For anything that might trip us up. She's wild and loose and excited. She takes my hand after rolling up the window, begging for me to warm her up. Her skin against mine stops time. The snow halts in mid-air. The road, pure black, freezes against an icy backdrop. I look at her and see the rest of our lives. She smiles, and her eyes light up, blue and free.

She asks me what we'll do if we see a cop. I tell her we won't, but I don't know. She presses me, and then I'm telling her the backup plan.

"We'll just drive like we normally would. Maybe for a few miles. Just until we can take one of these snow-covered side roads. They lead nowhere, and no one would follow us."

I'm still holding her hand tight while I think about the map I studied over and over again. Derrick picked the spot. He told me it was the best place. Kyle couldn't know about it, so Derrick and I made a few test runs over the preceding days. Now, he's a few miles behind me in his dad's pickup. The winch on the front of the truck would come in handy if we got stuck in the snow.

I'm lost in thoughts of police chases and escapes when she leans over. The thickness of her bubble coat crinkles and pops as she moves. Her face is an inch from mine, her lips in my ear.

"I love you," Bre says.

I say it back and she kisses me while I'm trying to keep one eye on the road.

At first, she didn't want to do this. She didn't think I should either. But I knew I'd be doing it the minute Derrick asked me to help. I tried to explain it to her, and after a while I think she got it. At best, it'd be fun—something I'd always remember, no matter how stupid. At worst, Kyle would still have his car and no insurance money. She said if I was going to be stupid, she was going to come along. And now, I know she likes it. The rush. The danger.

Still, I feel guilty. I don't need this. I need her.

"Should we forget about this, turn back?"

She laughs at the thought and says we've committed to it. "And when you commit to something, Thomas," she says, holding out her bare ring finger and waving it in front of me, "you better follow through."

The snow comes down thicker, and I welcome its cloaking blanket. As if the white of the Celica under the white snow makes us invisible. The relief slides beneath my chest, and I breathe easier.

The plan is simple. I take the car to the spot Derrick and I selected. Derrick follows behind to pick me up. Kyle calls the Celica in as stolen. We split the insurance money.

She's looking out the window when she asks, "What do you think about at night before you fall asleep?"

"Just you."

She smiles into her chest before laughing and calling me a liar. We laugh together and watch the white-capped pine trees fly past in a blur.

We met in class, but it wasn't until I had seen her around town that I finally asked her out. I had barely gotten my learner's permit, but I promised her when I had my license I'd drive her somewhere special.

She kicks her faux fur boots up on the dash, and I follow the lines of her legs with my eyes, smooth as the mounds of snow outside the Celica's windows. I reach out and tickle her thigh. Her giggling sends chills down my spine, and I realize how much I want to stay in that car forever.

That's when I see the Highway Patrol cruiser fly by in the opposite direction.

"Fuck," she yells, leaning forward so she can try to track the cruiser in the side mirror.

"It's fine, don't worry."

"That's a cop, Tommy."

"I know, but we're OK."

"You don't know that."

"There," I say, pointing at a gap in the road, a turn-off to the right.

She takes a few breaths, looks at me as I slow the car, then smiles. "Shit."

I know Derrick will see the Highway Patrol cruiser. I'd told him beforehand that if we saw a cop, I would duck down the first road I could find and wait things out. I'm hoping he'll find this road as I feel the Celica sliding along the snow beneath its tires. The road is narrow and doesn't look like anyone has driven it in months. It's similar to the place Derrick and I chose to ditch the car.

We'll drive the Celica far enough out that no one should find it. Then we'll destroy it. Derrick has a couple baseball bats, a sledgehammer, razor blades, a tire iron, and a few jack stands in the bed of the pickup. I figure we could just leave the car out there and no one will find it. There's nothing out there. No trails, no buildings, just an access road leading nowhere. But Derrick and Kyle want to make sure the car is totaled in case it's found.

She slaps my knee as she laughs. I laugh in spite of everything. I ignore what will happen if that cop pulls us over and think about Bre and me and our life together.

We're never leaving. That's the plan to keep us from falling apart. We'll go to university next fall and never have to leave the city. I don't see how any of it will change. The world might crack and break and split apart at the seams, but I know she and I will be wrapped around each other, holding on until the end.

When we're sure the cop isn't following us, she asks, "What would you do if he came after us?"

"I'd run. I'd press the gas as hard as I could and hope we made it."

"Tommy," she says, sliding as close as she can to me, right up against the center console. "Pretend."

She licks her lips and flicks her eyebrows up and down until I agree. I grin into the windshield and step on the gas. The front wheels lose traction at first, and we slide to the right, but soon they grip onto something, and we rocket down the lonely old road.

I remember her in math class sometime after we started dating. She's smarter than me, but in that class she had let me feel like I always had the answer before her. The truth is, I never had the right answer.

Even now, I know this isn't the right answer for her. For me.

She bangs her hands off the roof and yells. "Drive, Tommy. Drive."

The snow lets up, and I lose myself in the gray clouds above. The light reflects off the clouds and skips across her freckled face. She yelps with joy as we bounce across large rocks and old fallen tree branches. The road is washing away under an ocean of snow.

The forests and mountains outside Flagstaff are beautiful and sad, the perfect balance. A small bit of sadness within the beauty of a moment or a person or a life is what keeps us going. For me, the sadness is the occasional fleeting belief that she's nothing more than a figment of my imagination. That I'll wake up one morning, cold and alone.

On cue, she reaches over and massages my shoulder and neck. I sink into her fingers, I feel our bodies melt away. It's not me and her in that car. It's us.

The front wheels crank left, and we slide forward. It's all I can do to keep the car on the road, but somehow I get it to straighten out. She laughs at the adventure of it all, and I wonder how much longer we can keep this up.

I look over and see she's still enjoying the thrill of the fake chase, so I start making police siren noises and try to push the Celica a little faster in the snow. I see branches kicking up to either side of the car, powder pluming just beyond the rearview mirror, and her smile flashing a white brighter than any snow could match. Her cheeks dimple, and she grabs the base of the window to help keep her in the seat.

I met her family a while back. Her mom is a kindergarten teacher, and her dad is a butcher. She has a brother who will be starting high school when we go off to college. They creep into my mind as I'm struggling with the steering wheel. They love me like their own. They love the idea of me. They love that I love their daughter so much.

We're far enough down the road that I ask her if we should turn around and find Derrick. I ask her if we should get back on track. She doesn't hear me, or she chooses to ignore me.

"What would you say to me if this was—" She thinks for a second. "If this was our final stand, if the law was bearing down on us and we were looking at life behind bars?"

I laugh. "What are we, Bonnie and Clyde?"

She shrugs and smiles back at me.

"All right, Bonnie," I say in my best 1940s gangster voice. "I'll tell you everything."

I tell her about the children I want to have with her, and about the house we'll own. I tell her about our jobs, and I tell her about our life outside of work. I tell her we won't be those couples who stop having sex as we get older. I tell her we will talk to each other late into the night, discussing our day, discussing life, discussing our future. I tell her there's not a single thing in the world that could take her from me.

That's when I feel the back end of the Celica slide. I'm holding the steering wheel as tight as I can. My foot comes off the gas, hoping to slow us down. I don't dare to tap the brakes, but I can't keep the Celica from spinning.

I see the look on her face while trying to find a point in the road to focus on. Terror has stripped everything from her skin. Her eyes are wide. She's screaming as the Celica spins. We hit something, and the back of the car lifts off the ground. I close my eyes and try to block it out. Try to think about something else.

I was scared to death the first time we kissed. We were in her room, and she was begging me to kiss her, but I was worried about her parents. She finally snuck in and stole the kiss. I fell into it. I knew then that I wouldn't want to kiss anyone else for as long as I lived.

We land upside down for just a second before the Celica hits another branch and starts to cartwheel. I look over and see she's not wearing her seatbelt. I wish I had noticed. I want to ask her why she didn't put it on before we left.

I see her eyes squeeze shut. Then she's gone. Her seat is empty. I'm bouncing around, my head hitting the steering wheel, the door, the seat. The night surrounding us is whiter than it was before. I think it might be more snow, but I realize I just can't focus. Everything has blended into one spinning circle.

The car skids to a stop on its roof. I'm dangling in my seat, my head bleeding. Aside from the blood, I'm all right, I think. I look over, and her seat is still empty. I close my eyes and beg that it's a mistake, but when I open them again, she's still gone. I unbuckle my seatbelt and fall to the ceiling. I want to think about anything besides what I'm thinking.

Her skin shone under the summer sun on her parents' deck this past summer. We spent the entire last summer sitting on that deck after playful dips in the pool. I'm forcing the memory as I wonder if I'll get to see her skin like that again, wondering if I'll get to see her smile. She never wore a bikini when we swam, always a one-piece. Too embarrassing, she would say. She doesn't know how beautiful she is.

I crawl out through the shattered driver's side window and slide across the snowy, oiled ground. I don't know where she went. I can't find her. I search the hills of snow all around the road. Nothing. I'm spinning around on my hands and knees begging for a glimpse of her.

Then I see her.

It's dark, but I know it's her. I stop moving and look away. It's black all around me. I can't even see the snow anymore. It reminds me of the darkness of a movie theater right before the film rolls.

On our second date, I took her to an R-rated movie. Neither of us was seventeen yet, but I wanted to sneak her in. I bought tickets for a PG-13 comedy, and she seemed excited to see it. But when we crossed the threshold beyond the ticket-taker, I ducked us into the other movie. She laughed and let me have my fun. After the movie, she grabbed my hand and took me down the hall to the theater we originally should have gone to. The next showing of the PG-13 movie was about to start.

"Thank you, kind sir," she said, smiling. "Now you can suffer through my movie."

She takes everything in stride, and as worried as I am, I think she'll laugh this off one day too. Only, as I'm looking at her, I know that's not true. She never left the Celica. She'd been thrown into the back seat, but her neck looks weird. It looks wrong.

I don't know why I can't focus. Everything reminds me of something. Her neck, how I'd trace the line of it with my index finger while we sat together. Smooth and soft. The taste of it, warm and salty.

I crawl closer. Her head is lying on the ceiling, her body folded up above her, resting against the side panel inside the car. Her neck is tilted to the left, at an angle that doesn't make sense. She's not bloody, but she's not there. Her eyes are open, staring at me. The color has already left her, and a sort of gray has settled in. I know she can't see me, but I wave, trying to get her attention. I wave just like she used to wave at me.

When I got my first car, I picked her up for school every day. Even though she knew I was coming, she waved like a mad woman from the curb outside her house as I drove down the street. I can still see her bouncing up and down, her hair flopping back and forth, backpack banging against the small of her back, arm waving above her head. And every time she climbed in the car, she'd tell me she didn't think I'd stop. I'd tell her she could stop a train with just her smile, so she never had to worry about me passing her by.

The shock is coming in bursts. I stop waving, and I'm trying to convince myself that she's still alive. That she can be saved. I search for my phone but can't find it anywhere. I want to crawl into the car and be with her, but I'm afraid of hurting her more. I try to stand, but fire ignites in my stomach and rises through my throat. I'm puking all over snow that melts too quick at my feet and thinking about the last time she and I drank together.

I never wanted to admit it, but she held her liquor better than me. We didn't party like the other kids. We would stay in, wait for her parents to go to sleep, then sneak sips of wine and bourbon. The nights we got really drunk always ended with me puking in her backyard and her laughing and dancing around me. No matter how sick I got, I always knew that's how I wanted life to be.

I'm spinning in circles again, looking around. Something can fix this. Something can help. But there's nothing but white and dark sky, and my own screaming. She shouldn't be alone. I walk back to the side of the car and lie down next to the back window. I'm sliding as close as I can, my hand stretched out, not daring to touch her.

I gave her a ring once. Not an engagement ring, of course. Not a promise ring, either. I told her the promises we made to each other didn't require a ring. The ring I gave her was just a simple thank you for her being her. A present just because. It was sterling silver, nothing special. But I never saw her take it off.

I'm staring at that ring now.

I realize we're alone. Derrick's not coming. He wouldn't have known exactly what turn I had taken. I don't know what we'd been thinking. All this for a thrill. For a couple hundred bucks, at best.

I could walk. I might find the main road again, might find help. But there's no one who could help us, who could save her.

I'm not leaving. I'm staying with her forever. The snow feels warm beneath me. She looks cold. I don't think I can slide beneath the crushed metal and jagged glass to get inside with her, but I'm trying. If I can be next to her, with her, it'll be better. It's too tight.

I slide back, look around. Fall to the ground. If I can't crawl in through the back, I'll get back into the front. Be with her that way. I lay across the roof inside the Celica, my head tilted to the side enough to see her. Not close enough. I roll onto my stomach and crawl into the back. My head next to hers, I finally take her hand. I kiss her cheek, close my eyes. And I wait.

I wait for the snow to stop, for the air to warm. I wait for Bre to wake up and smile at me and steal my breath. I wait for someone to come and tell me it's all going to be alright. But no one is coming. So I'll stay with her. I'll wait.

SOLID LINES

At one hundred and twenty miles per hour, the dashed lines between lanes become solid. The entire highway freezes under a black canvas. When I get there, I always picture myself as a painting of that moment. My taillights firing out behind the bike like a laser. The lines between the lanes blurred into a single stripe of white. Me leaning up against my bike. Part of it.

The throttle vibrates beneath my palm. When the light turns green, I'll pull back and I'll be gone. The cars to my right don't exist. They think they do. But when that light turns green, they'll be nothing but a memory.

Just like her. Just like tonight.

"Frankie," she said when she was at my apartment the other night, "this can't go on."

She's the only one I let call me Frankie. Heather can get away with that.

"Why not?" I'd asked. I have asked her that same question every time since we split.

"You know why."

"Him?"

"No, me."

I shook my head when she said it, but maybe it's always been about her. Not me. Not her boyfriend. I don't know. All I know is that I'm nineteen, and I've got a hole in my chest that can only be healed by the road.

I can almost hear the traffic light change. I twist my wrist back, and the bike roars. I let the clutch pop away from my fingers and lean forward to keep the front wheel down. I'm gone. Forty-five miles per hour in two seconds. Sixty in four seconds. I'll slow down before the onramp, but with any luck that'll be the last time.

My Triumph Daytona is my escape hatch. I hit eject when things are going bad, and I'll find myself racing down the highway, troubles falling behind me.

The onramp is my last chance to change my mind, but I never do. I always do this at night after she leaves. Only, tonight is different. It's worse.

The warm night air slides around me, wraps its arms around my waist, tries to keep up. The stars dotting the horizon bounce under the vibration of one thousand CCs. I merge onto the highway and pull all the way back on the throttle.

She wore those jeans the other night. The ones I hate. The ones I love. I wanted to stare at them all night, but I couldn't. I couldn't let my eyes focus on how tight they were. How they clung to her hips and stuck to her thighs. How I felt like if I touched them, I'd be touching her skin. No, I had to steal glances.

The highway is all mine. I see two sets of red taillights about to disappear. They rise up in front of me and blow past me on the right. Now, the highway is empty.

It's a mistake to try to rush the process of forgetting. Forgetting takes time. To forget, I have to think, and I think best at eighty-five miles per hour. I think best when the road slides beneath my tires, the engine humming between my knees, the asphalt unrolling ahead.

When Heather turned twenty-one, things changed. When I was the eighteen-year-old with a crush and she was the twenty-year-old with nothing better to do, we could be together. But when she could go to bars legally, when she could meet men and forget about boys, we could only be friends.

Friends who kiss. And more.

Two nights ago, we crossed the line again. We made out until she fell asleep. I waited for her to wake up and race off to her boyfriend. I know she wants something more. More than what she has with him. But she won't let that something more be with me.

Now, she's gone for good. So I ride. I let the wind guide me along a darkened highway dragstrip open just for me. I rode after the last night with her, the night after, and now I'm here again.

As the highway straightens and I'm confident I have at least a few miles of curveless road ahead, I release the handlebars. I sit up straight in my seat and rest my palms on my thighs. The bike hurtles forward. It doesn't mind that I've set it free to do what it wants. That I've given it control for a few moments.

At this speed, with my body riding higher in the seat, the wind punches in tight jabs. But the wind does something more than attack me. It reminds me that I'm real. As it pounds me and tries its best to toss me from the bike, it lets me know I'm here. I'm alive.

When she woke up the other night, she did what she always does. She checked her phone. She tilted her head, brown strands of hair falling below her left eyebrow, green eyes begging the sleep and alcohol away, and told me she was sorry. She's always sorry afterwards. I never am.

She hugged me, convinced me she had slept off the beer, and told me this was the last time. He'd ask her where she was. He'd yell at her. She'd make it all go away. I know exactly how she'd do it, but I don't want to. I can't see her with him. I only let myself see her with me. Like it was back then. When we were just having fun.

But she didn't just leave me that night, she left him too.

I lean forward and grip the handlebars, but they're not there. I see my hands in hers, like they were that last night with her. Like I want them to be forever. The taste of Heather's mouth still slides along my tongue. Her hair still tickles my neck.

Another car rises up in front of me, and I swerve into the right lane. Now it's behind me. It reminds me of how quick these nights pass. She's there, I'm happy, then she's gone. The only thing I am left with is the belief that she'll be back again. But now, after tonight, she's not coming back.

After I've had my fill of thinking, I'll erase it all. Clear things out. When it's time, I'll become more than a kid on a bike. I'll become a ghost, teetering on the edge of here and there.

With my hands pressed against the handlebar grips and my body pitched forward, the wind is once again just a passenger, no longer an attacker. No longer a reminder.

Tonight, I wish it were raining. I want the torture of tiny beads of water transforming into pellets, hitting my body at eighty-five miles per hour. That's the kind of pain I can take. It's not like what I have now. The pain I have now doesn't set in until she closes the door to my apartment behind her.

She told me she'd had enough. Not of me. Not of her boyfriend. Just all of this.

"I can't be here anymore," she'd said. "I hate the smell, the taste, the feel. I hate the heat and the dirt and the blood-red sky."

"I thought you loved the sunsets." I said, like an idiot.

"I'm leaving, Frankie. I'm going to California tomorrow. I'm going to stay with my aunt."

I can still feel what I felt when she said that. It's like a cut that scabs over only for you to get it hung on something.

Heather's always been a runner, but now she's running too far. To California.

I close my eyes long enough to remember my last night with her. That night, she came over for a movie. She wanted to watch something with me. Her friend. She left with the taste of beer and my tongue in her mouth.

In the past, it's been dinner. Or lunch, just the two of us. I've never cared what it was that we did as long as we did it together.

See, we don't always cross the line. Last week, she came over just to talk. And that's all we did. No kissing. No touching. Those nights are the worst because I just want to be close to her. I can never be close enough.

And now, she's gone for good.

It's 3am and downtown Tucson rises up a mile ahead. Modest skyscrapers with every third window or so lit yellow. Downtown tosses light across the highway as I pass. Now, there's nothing but road.

When it was just us, Frankie and Heather, I thought our future was laid out for us. Call it fate or destiny or whatever you want. We had a life ready and waiting. I saw an apartment together. Not an apartment she came to when she needed to feel loved by someone other than her boyfriend. I saw her lips on mine because they belonged there. Not just because that was her release for the night.

We had our time together. Just me and her. Maybe that's all we'll get, but I don't believe that. Even with her leaving, I know she loves me. I hear it in her voice when she speaks to me. I see it in the slight curve of her lips when she's trying not to smile at one of my jokes. I feel it when she playfully slaps my arm.

Her boyfriend probably loves her. It's impossible not to. Her laugh. Her eyes, inviting and comforting. The way she takes a single moment, ties you to it, and makes you feel like you and her are part of something bigger. But I don't care about her boyfriend. I don't care that she left him(?).

My front tire slips into a groove in the road, and the bike shudders. The handlebars fight against me. But soon I'm clear of it. It's a gentle reminder of the things that can go wrong on nights like this. Of the thin net keeping me from the pavement.

Everyone goes down. If you ride, you've gone down. You have to learn how close you are to your end every time you ride. Going down once was enough for me. I had gravel in my arms and legs for weeks.

Sometimes, she'd put her hand on my chest. She wouldn't say a word. She'd look at me, at my eyes and my mouth and my nose, and she'd smile. I'd like to see that smile again, even if I have to chase it.

I'm no longer in the city. I'm somewhere in the wide open desert between towns. The miles unwind behind me and creep ahead of me. I've never gone this far on a night like this. By now, I would have opened up, shed the pain under the speed of a full throttle. Tonight though, I think I'll ride forever.

Maybe I'll go until the sun comes up. She's worth that beating. Worth hours of riding just to forget the bad and remember the good. I'm not sure I'll need to. I can feel bits and pieces of the pain breaking off. Floating away. Disappearing into the night behind me.

We didn't date. There was no lengthy courtship. She kissed me one night outside a party. The next night, we were together. Talking and laughing. Soon, we were having sex. Then we were in love. We could get back there. One of these nights, she'll be sitting on a beach somewhere thinking of me, and she'll remember. Until then, I'll ride away the pain.

Now, I'm ready.

I dip my head behind the windscreen. The chin of my helmet touches the gas tank. The wind can't find me now as I pull back on the throttle. This is when I know the knot in my stomach and this stabbing pain in my chest will go away. Where I know she'll come back to me someday.

The bike shakes beneath me. One hundred miles per hour. If I dip too low in a turn, pull the handlebar too quick, take my eyes off the road in front of me even for a second, I'll go down. I think about the bike sliding out beneath me, my legs and arms and chest and back ripped across jagged asphalt. I think about my head bouncing until the visor shatters and the fiberglass cracks.

When I'm with her, I can't slow my heart. Sitting on the couch next to her. Watching her walk to the kitchen. Leaning against her in my car. Next to her in my bed. I try to recreate the feeling of my racing heart while cutting through the night atop my bike.

At one-twenty, my body shakes. I can't hear anything even though I know sound is erupting all around me, spilling across the road and barreling into me. The lines have gone solid. I can't pick out the stars along the horizon anymore. I can't tell what I'm passing. I'm going too fast for anything but simple reaction.

My heart slams against my chest. It reminds me how I feel when she's with me, not how I feel when she leaves. Everything else is caught in the wind that's desperately trying to find me. It's carried away into the black.

I can't ever forget it all, and I don't want to. She'll always be on my mind. But I can breathe now and it doesn't hurt. I can picture her without my chest tightening.

Then my mirror clips a car I didn't know was there. I slip into the next lane, the lines and tar and night melting into one. The bike wants to go. It wants to tilt and escape beneath my legs, leaving me alone to slide across the highway.

But I recover. I slow down. I ride for a few minutes at the speed limit, the sounds of the road audible once again. I catch my breath, and the pain comes back. Sure, I can come back out. Do this again. I can keep doing this as long as the pain is there. But it might never go away. And if it doesn't, I know the next thing I hit won't just be a close call.

I think about taking the next exit. That's what I'd normally do. Take an exit, turn around, head home. But the bike pushes me on. I think about going back to my apartment and the air leaves my lungs, my stomach folds up on itself. So, I'm still riding. Still heading west.

It's easy to convince myself I'll turn around when I'm ready, but I know that's not true. I'll keep riding. The sun will rise, the gas stations will come and go. And I'll keep riding. All the way until I make it to California. All the way until I make it to her. All the way until we are together again.

ONE THOUSAND HOURS FREE

I liked to steal free trial discs of America Online. Every Wednesday—that's when our block got the big delivery of junk mail—I'd grab my backpack, hop on my bike, and I'd flip open each mailbox in my neighborhood, rifling through bills and flyers and credit card offers until I found that little disc that would buy me a few more minutes online with him.

FrancisFordMustang.

Today, I wasn't sure I'd find one. I tore through the next-to-last mailbox on the street. Maybe AOL had given up on their marketing efforts for my neighborhood. The last few times I'd gone out, I found some of the weaker trials—the ones that were hardly worth my time. Twenty-five free hours. Fifteen free hours. I'd burn through those in a couple of days.

My index finger bounced, clicking a mouse that wasn't there as I slammed shut the mailbox. One more to go. No, fuck it. I'd skip dinner with Mom and Dad. I'd ride to the next neighborhood, clear them out. Wouldn't make a difference. Mom would still ask how my day was, never looking up from her plate of food to see I wasn't there. Dad, he'd pat the empty chair, thinking he was patting my shoulder. He'd tell me what he told me every night.

"Rus, you take that ASVAB test yet?"

Jesus, the ASVAB. From the second I stepped foot into the linoleum-lined halls of high school, my father wanted to know what I'd do in the Air Force.

"This is a military town, Rus," he'd say. "We're a military family."

I wiped away the sweat on my forehead, moved on to the last mailbox. When I was seven, I ran straight into that same mailbox while trying to catch a duck of a pass from my older brother. Denny thought he could play football, but we learned later he was more of a coke and meth kind of guy.

I imagined that football sailing through the blue sky, cutting through the heat waves, and landing perfectly in my arms. Denny smiling. Me smiling. Us hugging. But what really happened was I didn't see the mailbox, turned my face just as I ran into it, lost two teeth, and Denny stopped playing with me.

The mailbox, lid half-open, still stood a little crooked in the gravel set off from the sidewalk. I pulled the lid down, stuck my hand in without looking. I knew the feeling. You'd think it would be round, but it was square. All that packaging. They had to fit the words some battle-tested marketer had come up with.

"Try it now, then only $9.95 per month!"

Mom might have gone for that, but not Dad. Freshman year, I had asked if we could get AOL.

"What would you even do on the internet?" Dad had asked. "You need a job. Take that test, figure out what you're good at, then we can start talking with the recruiters soon. Remember Jurry? He's working the recruiting office here in town now, maybe I can talk to him."

Thoughts of the recruiting office and my father shrunk toward the horizon as I felt it. That square packaging, cellophane-wrapped and smooth in my palm.

"Don't be shit," I whispered. "Don't be shit."

I pulled the disc out, closed my eyes, shut the lid to the mailbox. When I opened them, I saw it. One thousand hours. Dad could dream of military aptitude tests, Mom could read the paper and send her love through the repetitive words of a family that had given up. And Denny, he could stay in his fucking room, sleeping off another high.

Me, I'd be chatting with FrancisFordMustang.

When I got home, I let my bike ghost-ride into the garage, watched it bang off the quarter panel of Dad's Buick, then went in through the front door, zipping my bag as I stepped into the foyer.

The house was absent the smell of black tea and coconut-scented candles. Mom and Dad must have car-pooled to work. He might have been retired, but he went straight back to the Air Force in a civilian role while Mom worked at the bank downtown. I stood, listening. Denny's snores bumped along the walls and crawled across the floor before dying at my feet. I smiled. My brother's low rumble may have provided a different comfort for me when I was small, but now, it let the tension slip from my neck.

I passed through the kitchen, went into my room, and turned on my stereo. Might have just been Denny in the house, and he might have been sleeping, but if he heard the modem, he'd tell Mom and Dad.

As Michael Jackson's *Black or White* pulsed from the speakers of my stereo, I ripped the packaging away from the AOL trial disc. I opened the CD tray on my Intel 386 and slid the disc in.

AOL booted up, and I checked the phone line. I had it buried under sheets along my wall. Still plugged in. The modem kicked on and carried AOL's electrical signal across the line. It provided a weird beat as MJ sang to me about how he was tired of this devil. Once I was connected and signed on as SandDevil83, I turned the music down.

Then, I searched for him. The one time I'd found him online in the middle of the day, he didn't respond to me. Every other time, he had his away message on. Today, it was a quote from the movie *Patton*:

God, how I hate the twentieth century.

He and I had joked about that quote a few months back. He, wanting something simpler, something less authoritarian than the current world in which we lived, thought we should go back to an earlier time. Me, reminding him that we were pretty damn close to the twenty-first century anyway, suggested he create a new world for himself.

I'd almost forgotten what drew me to him originally. His screen name in the chatroom. When I was eight, I saw *Patton* for the first time. Last year, two days after my fifteenth birthday, I'd seen *The Godfather*. After that, I watched every old movie Francis Ford Coppola made. For Mr. Littleton's history class, I wrote an essay about Coppola and his relationship with the Ford family. So, when I found this person online who had played on both Coppola and Ford, I had to know him.

And he wanted to know me too.

I smiled at the quote, but there would be no chatting now. I signed off before I could waste any more minutes of my one-thousand-hour score.

*

Mom and Dad didn't bother waking me when they got home. They didn't wake me when Denny threw up and choked on his own vomit. The smell of sizzling ground beef woke me up.

Before I went to the kitchen, before we settled into routine, I looked at my computer. I'd chatted with Lorraine a few times at first. Chatted with Bobby, who lived six houses down. Kids from school. Friends. Reminders that no one can see me no matter how often I see them. I haven't chatted with anyone but FrancisFordMustang for three months.

At dinner, Mom kissed the top of my head without peeling her eyes away from the day's issue of *Investor's Business Daily*. Becoming a manager at the bank meant she had to care more about the rolling tides of the market.

I sat next to Dad, and he asked me about school.

"It's summer, Dad."

"Right," he said. "No test then, I suppose."

"Where's Denny?"

"Oh, that poor baby is just too sick to eat," Mom said, finger running along the black printed stock symbols representing money we'd never have.

"I bet."

"Rus, he's sick. Okay?"

"Sure," I said to her. "The last time he got sick, he kicked me in the ribs until I gave up my wallet. So, you know."

"Russell James Young," my father said, taking a bite of his taco. "That's your brother you're talking about. He needs our help in getting better, so we'll help him. I expect you to do the same."

"You want me to help him? How about I go buy his next score, make sure he smokes so much he doesn't wake up? That's the kind of help you're looking for right?"

"Goddamnit, Russell," my father yelled. "I'm sick of this. That summer prep school? They're still taking applications. Why don't I get you in there. That'll get you ready for the Air Force." He looked back at his food and started eating again. "That'll teach you to talk about your brother that way."

The fucking prep school wasn't a prep school at all. It was a daycare for kids who had too much time on their hands during the summer. I looked away from my dad to my mom.

She wouldn't meet my eyes and didn't say a word. She didn't have to. She'd be mopping up Denny's puke, wiping his face later tonight. That spoke loud enough for her.

I looked at them not looking at me, then I shoveled my dinner into my mouth.

The tacos taste like shit, Mom. Oh, and Dad, Denny scores from Mr. Roberts just down the road, the guy you think is so smart, such a good influence on the neighborhood. I swallowed it all, just like I swallowed that overcooked meat.

I didn't see them after dinner. Dad liked to drink his tea and watch Tom Brokaw tell him how other people's lives were so much worse. Mom would take a bath and fall asleep in the tub with candles lit around her.

I went back to my room and waited.

An hour after I heard Mom check on Denny then head back into her room, I crept out into the hall. I moved toward their door, and I held my breath. They had a television in there, but it wasn't on. I waited. I listened. Then it came. Dad's snore.

If Dad was asleep, Mom was asleep.

We used to live by the train tracks. Back then, I could count on the evening train running straight to Mexico at about 11. That horn, that'd be a wonderful thing. Time it with the sound of the modem's whirs and beeps. But we moved after Denny's first overdose. Better neighborhood, a new chance, my Dad tried to convince us. But our last neighborhood wasn't broken. Denny was. Mom was. Dad was.

Fuck, I was.

In the living room, I grabbed two thick microfiber throw pillows from the couch. I was about to bring them back to my room, but Denny was standing in the hall, watching me. He'd once been twice my weight, but now I was a solid fifteen pounds heavier than him. But he was still taller. He was still quick. And he blocked my path when I tried to get by to my room.

"What do you want?"

"Heard you were bitching about me," he said, wiping sweat from his lip and forehead. "The fuck did I do to you?"

"Nothing, just let me by."

"You want to bitch about something, I'll give you a reason."

He shoved me back into the living room. I tripped and fell. He stood over me, eyes drooped but hard. He flared his nostrils, clenched his fists, then he stepped past me, sat on the couch, and held his knees to his chest.

I watched him for a minute, but I knew what came next. He'd tear open the kitchen drawers, looking for the foil, looking for a spoon. He'd have something stashed in his room. He always did, no matter what our mother thought.

I turned away from him and brought the pillows into my room. I locked the door behind me and stuffed a pillow on either side of the

386's tower. When I booted up and launched AOL, the muffled sound of the 56k modem connecting sounded more like an odd snoring than a kid with a stolen trial of AOL trying to find his friend.

My Buddy List greeted me. And there he was. The green dot next to his name, pulling me in like a bug to the lamps we'd put out when we went camping in Sedona before Denny graduated.

Before I could click on his name, a message window popped up. From him.

"Hi!"

I wrote back and told him I'd tried to find him earlier in the day. I laughed when he asked if I saw the away message.

"Best character from *The Outsiders*?" I asked him.

"C. Thomas Howell, hands down."

"No way."

"Ponyboy, man."

I'd once asked my father what he thought of Coppola. My dad laughed and said fiction and film were the things of dreamers. Irrational wastes of time. He would stick to the news, non-fiction, and his own family.

His own family. I didn't laugh then, and I didn't laugh now, remembering it.

"You're watching it all wrong," FracisFordMustang wrote.

"What do you mean?"

"Hard to explain. Wish I could show you. But you're watching that movie wrong. Otherwise, you'd know C. Thomas Howell is the best."

"I'd watch it with you," I typed.

He didn't reply for a long time, and my fingers danced across the keys of my keyboard, not typing but searching for something I could say.

"We could meet in the middle somewhere," he finally typed, quickly followed by, "LOL just kidding."

We'd talked about his house in El Paso and my school here in Arizona. We'd talked about the distance, about the differences of the desert there versus the desert here. We had even talked about how long MapQuest said it would take to make the drive.

But we'd never talked about this.

I almost typed "no," but then I remembered my dad, remembered the prep school.

"Where's the middle?" I asked.

"Somewhere in New Mexico."

"But where?"

"Lordsburg."

"I've never heard of that."

"It's cool."

"What movie would we watch first?"

He didn't say anything for a while again. Then, "What?"

"If I came out there."

I'd asked him once how old he was, and he told me he was forty-three. Same age as my dad. I sat back in my chair, listened to the house stretch its bones, creaking and popping. I didn't know his name. That mattered. But it didn't, really. I could talk to him about school, about the fucking ASVAB test that didn't mean shit, about how the Air Force was a cop out. I could talk to him about how Bobby started seeing Gina and stopped talking to me, about how Lorraine once thought I was into her and that weirded her out too much. I could talk to him about Denny. Fucking Denny.

"I think we'd start with *Peggy Sue Got Married*," he wrote. "It's funny enough."

"Nicholas Cage and Jim Carey."

"Right."

"But how?" I asked.

"How what?"

"How do I get there?"

After a minute, he sent me a link through the messenger window. I clicked it and the Greyhound Bus website popped up. I saw the address for the station downtown.

"It'll only be a few bucks to get to Lordsburg," he wrote.

"And from there?"

"I'll drive you to El Paso."

It'd be a quick drive with the things we would discuss. A conversation about the mechanisms of time travel in *Peggy Sue Got Married*. A discussion on the merits of military service or blue-collar work or white-collar work. Arts, challenges.

The coma my soul had been in for what felt like years wore off. Like waking up in a stark white hospital room marking the start of something new, I could move again. Breathe again. Live again.

"I've got enough for the ticket," I wrote.

"When would you do it?"

"Now."

"Now?"

"The schedule says there's a midnight bus. I can make that."

"If you want to, I can make it to Lordsburg in time to get you."

Just for the summer, I thought. Give my parents time to think. Maybe Denny would get his shit together too. Just for the summer. Just for a couple months.

"Let's do it."

"Great," he typed. "I'll meet you at the Lordsburg station tomorrow morning."

"We're doing this?"

"If you really want to."

"I do," I typed.

"When you're waiting in Lordsburg, look for an old Ford Mustang."

Of course.

*

I shoved as many clothes as I could fit into my backpack and walked the half-hour to the bus station. The clerk took my money, didn't ask my age, didn't give a shit.

On the bus, I watched the silhouettes of cactuses and trees wave their goodbyes. I saw the mountains fall away, replaced by jagged, beautiful hills of New Mexico. I saw a world open, spreading its arms and stepping out of the shadows.

My parents would be awake soon. They'd go and check on Denny, make sure he hadn't swallowed his tongue or died with a piece of foil in his hands. Then, they'd go to work. Disappearing was only momentous when discovered. But it might be days before my parents knew I was gone.

"He's probably studying up for his test," my dad might say.

"Maybe he's just thinking about how he can be nicer to Denny," my mom would chime in.

All the while, it would be Denny who discovered I was gone. He'd be looking for another quick score. Looking for money. And he would find my room empty.

The bus stopped too many times, the seats felt like they were made of rock, and every time a semi's Jake brake woke the person up next to me, he'd just stare at the side of my face. But we made it to Lordsburg.

The sun had been up for an hour or so, but the cool night air of the evening had not been burned away. I shivered on the bench outside the station, looking for an old Ford Mustang. The people getting off in Lordsburg cleared out. The people getting on were carried away. Soon, the station was empty.

But I waited. He'd come. He'd show up.

Peggy Sue Got Married then *Rumble Fish* then *The Outsiders*. We'd leave *The Godfather* for last. Had to. In between, we'd have meals and talks, and we would be people. Real people who cared what the other had to say.

Just as the sun had begun warming the day, a rusted Ford Mustang with a dented passenger door choked and coughed its way into the parking lot. The Mustang stopped in the lot right in front of me. I couldn't see the driver clearly, but I saw him lean across the seat and pop open the passenger side door.

Just for the summer, I reminded myself as I stood and walked to the car.

CLEAT CHASER

The gravel beneath her tires spit up and knocked against the wheel well. Her seatbelt stretched and sighed as she moved her body and searched for a parking spot. The single pop of the bad knuckle on her left hand echoed in the car.

It was all too loud. It wasn't loud enough.

Leah McColsky wanted the noise. The whole drive over, she'd been hoping to get inside the bar, let the music and the cheering and the conversations all around drown out her thoughts. Maybe then she wouldn't have to go through with what she was about to do. But even in the exacerbated noise chamber of the front seat of her rusted Buick Skylark, Leah couldn't shut off her mind.

She couldn't stop thinking about the dark room switch—the rape. And she couldn't stop thinking about how he did nothing about it.

She found a spot a few rows from the entrance. It was the only sports bar in Sahuarita, a little suburb of Tucson. Come Friday night, she'd heard it was the only place to be. It didn't hurt that they had a bona fide professional athlete pouring drinks. Patrick Murphy. He had a cup of coffee in the Majors, but that was enough. He got his face on a baseball card, could say he faced Ken Griffey Jr., and made just enough money to know how shitty life back here in Arizona was.

Leah killed the engine and sat there, staring at the brick and adobe building across the parking lot. It took her forty minutes to make the drive, and in that time, she changed her mind over and over thinking about her approach. She'd walk right up to the bar, ask if he remembered her. No, she'd wait it out, wait for him to close, corner him in the dark parking lot. She still didn't know which approach she'd take as she popped open her door and climbed out.

Winter in the desert struck you in the face like a cold backhand. The air smelled like a fire log soaked in rainwater, and the temperature made people forget where they were. Even the snowbirds were known to complain when December flipped to January and the night temps dipped into the teens. Leah sucked in a breath, blew it out, wished she could follow the warm vapor stream up into the clouds. But she needed to be here. She needed this.

She'd already made plans for the other players, but Pat, he had to be first. It helped that he was the only one who'd already washed out, who'd been forced from the game. It helped that he was relatively local. It didn't help that he wasn't in the room that night. Leah was more frustrated with him than angry. Confused, maybe.

She walked to the front door and stopped. It was late enough that she'd have no choice but to grab a stool at the bar. She had come in three or four times before in the previous weeks. Building courage. Scouting the layout. Didn't matter. She would sit where she sat, and she'd deal with this.

Leah opened the door, let the sounds pulse and snake across her skin up to her ears. She stepped inside and nearly threw up. He was there, across the room, pouring tequila into a shaker. It wasn't as if she didn't think about that night every day. She did. But seeing him in person brought it back with a level of clarity she hadn't experienced since it happened. Now, sitting at the bar, a fake smile stretched across her face, her mind traveled back to that shitty townhouse in Tortalita.

No, that's not where her mind went. It went to the days and weeks after. Her friends asking why she hadn't called the police. Her friends asking if she was sure it happened. Some friends even going so far as to suggest Leah was a cleat chaser, that she wanted it. But Leah hadn't even known what a cleat chaser was when she went to the minor league game at the old stadium in Tortalita.

She had been sitting by the bullpen when Miguel Santiago found her in the crowd. It was during a night game years ago—before the

Single-A team moved to some small town in Texas. Miguel had been looking for someone, anyone. Leah knew that now, but she felt special then. When he found Leah, he stopped searching, wrote something on a baseball, and tossed it up to her. It was a phone number and a question.

Dinner?

Focus, Leah told herself, letting the sound from the bar hit her ears once again. The thoughts popped and faded like a sparkler on a summer night. Then, she caught him looking. Pat Murphy, older and grayer, but just as tall and lean. If he hadn't still looked like a pitcher—which he did—the memorabilia behind the bar made it hard for anyone to forget.

The local kid who'd made it big. Newspapers, framed. Signed baseballs. A pair of cleats on a wood shelf. All Pat, everywhere.

Leah held Pat's stare, but Pat ducked his head, looked at the tap, then crouched behind the bar top. She walked past the general seating and found an empty stool. Pat's head bounced as he did whatever he was doing behind the bar. He stayed down there a long time, so Leah sat and waited.

When he finally came back up, he looked like he might fall over. She smiled, but didn't say anything. Leah still wasn't sure how she'd handle this meeting. Before she came in, she wondered if Pat would even remember her, but seeing him now made it clear. He remembered everything.

"What're you drinking?" he asked her, avoiding eye contact.

"Miller," Leah said. "Leave the tab open."

She watched him run her credit card, grab a Miller from the cooler beneath the bar. He handed it to her and turned to another customer without a word. He looked tired, but so did everyone else she knew. He might be tired, might be older, she thought, but he was still the same guy she passed on the way out of that house years ago the morning after it happened. The same guy who had been there that night, just outside the door. Doing nothing.

"You own this place?" she asked Pat.

Pat finished pouring a beer for a customer at the end of the bar and came close enough to hear her. "What's that?"

She nodded toward the wall. "Looks like you own this place. Is it yours?"

Keep it casual. Play dumb. That's the approach, she decided.

Pat looked at all the stuff on the wall. He stayed facing that direction for longer than necessary. When he turned around, he said, "No, they just put that stuff up there because people like to remember."

"You were a pitcher, huh? Any good?"

Pat shifted his weight from one foot to the other, moved the clean glasses behind the counter around. The whole time, his eyes held the wood grain of the bar top.

"Yeah, I was alright, I guess. Starter mostly."

Leah leaned back a bit, re-reading the situation. Maybe he didn't recognize her. He hadn't called her out on knowing the answers to these questions. She took a drink from her longneck Miller and smiled.

"Make it to The Show?"

"Yep. Not for long, though."

"Making it's all that counts. No matter the costs, right?"

Pat's smile was forced, like the skin around his mouth fought against the muscles that demanded a grin. Then, he was gone. As if someone had called him over, he disappeared to the other end of the bar. But he just stood there, cleaning an already clean glass.

He knew who she was. He knew what this was about. Leah took another drink, shook her head, then called Pat back over.

"Need something else?" he said when he slowly made his way back.

"I still dream about you, you know?"

Pat grabbed a bottle opener then stopped moving. He looked at her. "Excuse me?"

Leah held his eyes. She wasn't smiling anymore. "I have this dream where you kick down the door." She laughed. "Stupid, huh?"

Pat didn't say anything, but he didn't look away.

"Wanna get out of here when you close up?" Leah asked.

Pat held up his left hand and pointed to the ring. "I'm married."

"I'm not trying to fuck you, Pat."

As soon as she said his name, Leah's stomach untied itself. The hesitation and nerves that told her to run away were gone. She wasn't sure if he'd go with her, but she had asked. She'd taken the first step.

Leah had been attending a support group for women who'd experienced sexual assault for a few years now. She used to go to the meetings weekly, now she was content if she made it once a month. One thing that stuck with her was the idea of confrontation. She was certain they didn't mean literal confrontation, but that's what she needed.

Pat stood there in front of Leah, avoiding her eyes, thinking. Then he said, "So you remember me?"

"I do."

"Then why would you want to get out of here with me?"

"Just to talk."

She didn't actually want to talk about it. Never did. Even in her support group, she shied away from telling people what happened to her until it finally just spilled out.

Miguel had seemed so nice. So respectful. He took Leah out to dinner twice before he asked her to the party. Never made a move before that night. At the party, they drank. A lot. She wanted him, he wanted her. It was perfect. Until she woke up the next morning and realized what had happened.

"I don't think that's a good idea." Pat picked at a chipped section of the bar. "Plus, there's nowhere to go."

She wished he had put on weight or had some indication that karma had caught up with him. But he was thin, looked good, had a life, and was married.

"Besides, I've got a little girl I need to get home to," he continued.

Married with a daughter, apparently.

"We'll make it quick. I just want to talk. There's a convenience store across the street. I'll buy you a beer over there."

Pat looked up at the clock. "What would we talk about?"

"You know what we'd talk about."

Staring at the tap to his left, Pat ran his finger along the bar.

"Please," Leah said.

There was a power in confrontation. In addressing the demons and asking them why. For a while, after it happened, Leah let the demons hammer her into the ground. She didn't go out. She started listening to the things her friends were saying. She wondered if she really did deserve it.

But she found the support group. She took her life back by finding things to give her power. Confrontation was an important part of finding power. And if things fell apart with Pat, she'd never have a chance with the other two.

"All right," Pat said, blowing air from puffed cheeks. "But we've gotta make it quick."

For the remainder of the night, Pat left Leah alone. And she left him alone. She sat on her stool, staring at the television above the bar play *SportsCenter* on a loop, remembering.

Pat had his headphones in that night. Maybe, he'd been so lost in the music that he didn't understand what was happening. But Miguel would have had to have come back out past him. Miguel would have brought Billy and Donovan past the couch and into the room. Pat should have seen that. He had been right there, right outside the room.

Leah had talked to Pat for most of the night before Miguel was done socializing and ready to fuck. Pat loved baseball. He loved the desert. He dreamed of playing in Phoenix for the Diamondbacks so he could spend half his season in Arizona. She had reminded him he was already spending half his season in the desert with his minor league club, but he laughed that off. "It's not the same," he'd said.

Leah realized she was one of the only people left in the bar. She looked at the time. Almost two in the morning. For a minute, Pat came near Leah as he cleaned. When he stopped, he looked at her for a long time.

"Don't get lost in my eyes, Pat. You're married, remember?"

He looked away. "Just thinking."

"Me too."

Pat went to the register and counted the drawer. When he was done, he counted again. Keep counting, she thought. I'm not going anywhere.

Leah knew how much it would hurt. She knew how stupid this might be. Her best bet was moving on and forgetting the whole thing ever happened. Except, that wasn't her best bet. She'd never forget that night, so the best she could hope for was understanding it.

After Pat moved the money from the register to a green deposit bag and placed the bag into the safe in the back office, he came back out to the bar. He rubbed his eyes and sighed.

"You ready?" Leah asked.

Pat looked up, gave her a half-smile. "Sure."

They walked out together and Pat locked the door behind them. The night had grown colder. Leah pulled her coat closed around her, hugged herself. They walked to Pat's Ford, where he flipped down the tailgate.

"I'll be back," Leah said.

She crossed the parking lot to the convenience store. She bought two bottles of shit beer and carried them back out in brown paper bags. Pat was sitting on the tailgate of his truck when she came back across the parking lot. She watched Pat's breath escape him—little puffs of white air against the cold—and wondered if she was doing the right thing. She let out a long sigh and watched her own breath slip away from her into nothing.

She knew all three men who had taken her. It started and ended with Miguel, but there were two others. She didn't remember it all, but she remembered enough of it the next morning. She huddled in the corner of the bedroom on the floor while listening to men laugh and crash dishes together somewhere else in the townhouse. It wasn't clear how it had happened, but she knew it did.

Pat had simply been the kid outside the door that didn't stop it. Maybe she didn't need to talk to him. He wasn't a stupid kid anymore. Neither was she. She could go straight to Miguel—if she could get past his agent and the team employees that kept fans at a distance. Only, she wasn't a fan. She was something worse. A victim.

Leah handed a beer to Pat and sat on the tailgate next to him. "Miguel's putting together a pretty decent career."

Pat nodded. "He is."

"Miss it?"

"Playing?"

"Yeah." She took a long sip of beer.

"Sometimes."

"How'd it end?"

Pat took a drink, wiped his mouth. "I sucked."

Leah laughed in spite of herself. "That'll do it."

"No joke. They have that shot of me pitching to Griffey up on the wall in the bar, but what you don't see it what happens when I deliver that pitch. He fucking crushes it 428 feet over the right field wall."

"But you made it."

"I made it."

Leah watched the moon duck behind a thin cloud. A coyote barked somewhere in the desert east of the plaza.

"I thought Miguel was a nice guy. I thought it was normal, you know?"

Pat nodded and kept drinking. "He was an asshole."

"Was?"

"Probably still is."

"Yeah." Leah looked at Pat. He stared straight ahead, his head frozen in place. As if moving it would be an indictment for the role he played on that night.

She saw him like she'd seen him back then. Young, confident, the world opening up to him. With his headphones in, eyes sagging, she and Miguel had passed him. He'd nodded to her on the way by, and she smiled at him. She'd drank too much. Leah recognized that now, but Miguel had a private stash in the room. When he took her into the bedroom, she and Miguel took shots for another twenty minutes. Then, they got naked.

"I've never told my wife," Pat said.

"What?"

"My wife," he said, shaking his head. "I never told her about that night."

"What would you tell her?" The beer she was drinking suddenly made her think of the shit they had at the party that night, so she put it down.

"I don't know, the truth, I guess?"

"Which is what?"

Pat shook his head.

"It's probably smart that you didn't tell her."

"You think?"

"What would she think of you if she knew?" Leah asked. "What would your daughter think? Your friends?"

"Nothing good, I'm sure."

"Then why'd you let it happen?"

The truth was, Leah could have been wrong. She'd spent so long convincing herself that she was, that Patrick Murphy had no idea what happened behind that bedroom door. But they had a name for it—the dark room switch. The team had to have talked about it. That Miguel was able to get two guys to join in with such little effort meant others knew. Including Pat. And he'd been outside the door. He'd watched them all enter that room. He'd known she was in there, drunk, naive.

Pat didn't answer her question. Fuck it, Leah thought, and grabbed her beer. She picked it up and held it out toward Pat's.

"Cheers," she said.

"What?"

"A toast to unanswered questions."

Leah finished her beer, and Pat finished his. She let her bottle roll backward in the truck bed. Pat held his empty between his legs, shoved his hands into the pockets of his hoodie. The frost began its early morning strike. The saguaro in the distance sparkled under the ice forming on its needles. Leah shivered and started to climb off the tailgate. But Pat stopped her.

"I didn't stop it because I was a coward. Still am."

"What were you afraid of?"

Pat sniffled, and Leah wasn't sure if it was because of the cold or because he felt bad. He looked at her and said, "Losing everything."

"Baseball." She looked away.

"Baseball was everything. And I didn't know what would happen if I did something. If I went against the grain. I'm not excusing it, I'm really not. But you wanted an answer, and that's it. I was afraid for myself."

"I was afraid for myself too," Leah said. "The next day, when I couldn't figure it out, you know?"

He nodded, but he wouldn't look at her anymore.

"What did you see? What did you know?"

"I'd heard of it. Didn't think it was something that really happened."

"The dark room switch."

"Yes," Pat said. "At first, I just saw Miguel take you to the room, and that was cool. But then, when Miguel came out, a smile on his face and a finger to his lips, I was confused. When two of the other guys—"

"Billy O'Bannion and Donovan Gorder," Leah reminded him.

"Right. When Billy and Donovan followed Miguel back into the room, unbuckling their pants, I felt sick."

"So, you didn't do anything to stop it. What'd you do instead?"

Pat squeezed his eyes shut and sighed. "I put my headphones on, laid down on the couch, and went to sleep."

"You were still there the next morning, on that couch."

"I know. I saw you leave."

For a few minutes, they let the occasional rumble of a truck on the freeway in the distance keep them company.

Leah tried over the years to put herself in Pat's position. If she knew what was going on behind that door, she thought she knew what she would have done. She would have kicked the fucking door down if she had to. But now, sitting on the tailgate with the one person who could have rescued her, she wasn't sure what she would have done.

It was never Miguel and the other two that she thought of as the days and weeks and years went by. It was always Pat. She knew the questions she'd ask the others, but she hadn't understood Pat at all. Now, she was a lot closer to understanding.

"How often did that happen?" Leah finally asked.

Pat shook his head. "I don't know. I never saw it again after that night, but that doesn't mean they didn't do it without me knowing."

"Is that just how it is with you guys? With baseball players?"

"I hope not."

"Me too."

"But I don't know," Pat said.

Miguel became a free agent that winter. Leah had been following his career. His rise through the minors. His Major League debut. His All-Star appearance. If she was ever going to confront him, it had to be this winter, while he was still unsigned. While he was most approachable, living in his ridiculously large home in Las Vegas.

Pat let the bottle fall from between his legs. It clinked off the gravel but didn't break. "I'm sorry, Leah. I really am. I don't deserve to have this chance, but I'm glad you came by. I'm glad I could look you in the eyes and say this. I'm so, unbelievably sorry."

"Thank you," she said and looked away.

Leah tightened her arms around her body, fighting a chill that spread through her body. Then she let her arms drop to her side, and she slid off the tailgate. He'd just been a stupid kid. She'd been a stupid girl. Now she knew.

"I forgive you, Pat."

Leah walked away from Pat's truck. She was almost to her car when he called after her.

"Are you going to be alright?"

She didn't say anything, just smiled and climbed into her car. As she pulled out of the parking lot, Pat continued sitting on the edge of his tailgate, looking at the ground.

THE DISSOCIATIVE PROPERTY

I've never met my employer. The application process was electronic. Communication via email. I took tests online and at a contracted medical facility. Stress tests, physical tests, writing tests, and the most important test.

The psychological test.

I had taken tests like that in the past and I remembered the key was making sure you didn't change your answer when the question was asked again with different phrasing. Or, maybe that was a personality test.

Regardless, I passed.

"The dissociative property results were through the roof," the congratulatory email said. That email was signed by an Employee ID but not a name. Their formula for calculating this property—a property they seemed to have invented—was never revealed.

That's the way it went. Nameless co-workers and bosses, reveling in my dissociative score. That's why they paid for the office in the little shopping plaza near my house. Only the best for me, they said.

It's not a great office. It has a single window covered by broken mini-blinds. But the company sprang for a microwave and a miniature refrigerator. Because of my personality. Because I could do the job.

They told me that's why I keep getting raises as well. They needed someone like me for so long, and now they had me.

"And we're not letting go," Employee ID 231156 said as a joke in an email a while back.

I'm not feeling very dissociative, though. My job is boring. So boring that I've begun talking to my spreadsheets. Which is, of course, all my job is. Spreadsheets and online job board postings. Maybe a newspaper classified ad here and there if the bosses are feeling nostalgic.

I work for Hamilton Fishing Enterprises, the deadliest workplace in America. But I don't experience any of that from my office in the shopping plaza. I just see the spreadsheets. I see rows turn orange thanks to distant mouse clicks on the shared file. And I see rows turn red.

It's the numbers in the colorless rows I've been talking to. And I suppose that's a problem. I suppose that undermines the purpose of my job, the reason I'm tucked away in a remote office, away from company headquarters, away from the fishermen and women who make up my spreadsheets in sorted numerical columns.

I'm where I am because of what I do. What needs to be done. Commercial fishing is the most dangerous job in the country. And Hamilton doesn't have a great record. But they have to fill openings. And those openings come from the deaths and serious injuries of existing employees.

But the people who know these men and women who go out on the seas cannot be expected to post a job opening. They can't be expected to ignore their emotions, set aside their sadness, and ask for applications. That's what the bosses tell me. They say it's too difficult.

But someone has to do it. So, I'm here. Doing just that.

"George, things have been going a little too well," I say to a row in my spreadsheet containing Employee ID 245678. This number just felt like it was a George.

I checked the rows one more time. No new oranges or reds since two weeks ago when I had to post four job opportunities all in the same day. George felt bad on that day, so I felt bad as well.

"How are things out there? I worry and wonder, George. I think if I'm not posting a new job that—"

I can't even say it. He knows what I worry about. I've been talking to him for a month now. It seems like it happened all at once, but there were days, maybe weeks, where I'd look at his row, I'd look at his number, and I'd almost say something. But I didn't. Until last month.

I flip over to the job board. Part of my job is to sift through the applications, toss the spam, forward the good applications to the bosses. These people, I assume, get to know the bosses. They learn their names, their faces. If they're hired, they learn the personalities of the bosses. But not me. And that's alright. I've got George now.

Even if I'm not supposed to. Even if I might lose George to a colored row.

"Ten new applications, George," I say, flipping back to my spreadsheet. I like to address him directly, not behind another browser window. "Can you believe that? We'll have those positions filled in no time. Get you some help out there on those rough waters."

The day passes. Lunch is a frozen pasta meal with an orange juice. Then I go home. It's been a year of this. Go to work, look at the spreadsheets, post jobs, go home, eat alone. But now, I've got George. Through him, I can leave that shopping plaza in the desert behind. I can be on the seas, working with George and the others. Seeing the world. But tonight, it's different. Tonight, I don't need to go anywhere because George has agreed to come over for dinner.

I make meatloaf and sit down with George across from me. He's thankful for the meal.

"You wouldn't imagine the shit they feed us out there on the water," he says.

He eats like—well, like a man who's been at sea for weeks. But I notice he hasn't touched the bottle of beer I set in front of him. I start to ask him about it, but then I remember. It's not real. George is not there. He's a number. His name probably isn't even George.

I shake the thought from my mind and force the imagination.

I imagine George telling me a story of their last outing. Two men had to be brought below deck after a rope came loose and sliced through their hands.

"So, will they show up orange?" I'm thinking about my spreadsheet. Thinking about the job. It's always about work. Stupid.

George shakes his head. "Nah, they're fine. They were back at it the next day. No problem."

I ask George about his family and he tells me he has two sons. He tells me he wouldn't wish this job on them if it were the only job in the world. He would want his sons to take to crime, to rob people before they ever worked the sea.

I think about the red rows in my spreadsheet and I understand. We shouldn't have to think about the bad stuff, so I make a joke about the sea.

"Hey, George," I say. "What do you get when you mix the ocean and the state of Colorado?"

"What?" he asks.

"Sea-Weed, man."

George falls off his chair laughing. It's nice to have a friend.

The night goes on like that for a couple hours, and then I'm tired. And then George is gone. And soon I'm asleep.

A new one went orange overnight. Employee ID 237890. I'm sitting in my office, the sun barely up, the morning traffic hardly making any noise outside. I should have slept in. I had a late night hanging out with George. I look at his row in the spreadsheet and smile at the memory of the stories he told me.

Then I look back to 237890's row. Shit.

Serious injuries are just as bad as death as far as the company is concerned. I get it. It means monetary settlements, newspaper reports, PR spins. All the things I don't handle. But it also means hiring, which I do handle.

I flip over to the job board. I've got a template for this type of thing. Makes life a lot easier when you're posting anywhere between 50 and 100 jobs per year.

The job is posted. They go up that quick. An orange line or a red line, and that person's job is ready for the vultures to pick apart within a day.

I scan the spreadsheet, find George's ID. Still colorless.

As the day drags on, I flip on the ceiling fan and watch its blades spin in a slow circle. I feel the musty air pushed down by the motion. I smell the dust kicking off the blades. Then, I make some bagel bites for lunch. I grab a Sprite and take my bagel bites to my desk and eat.

As I eat my lunch, I think about forgetting George. If I could talk to someone else, maybe I could. But I don't have anyone else. Mom's in the home, Dad's gone. There is no one else. Maybe that's why I got this job. Maybe that's why my dissociative property was so attractive. Maybe I was the dissociative property. Companies have "properties." That's what they call them. I think about those huge media companies I've read about. They have their film properties and their television properties. Perhaps Hamilton had me—their dissociative property.

I pull the string on the mini-blinds and raise them for the first time since I'd been working in that office. Sunlight bounces off my gray desk and into my eyes. I squint and look out across the shopping center plaza. Chrome and glass and blacktop. And people.

They walk from their cars to stores in the shopping center. Those coming from the grocery store carry bags, plastic and paper. They place them in trunks of cars. They talk on phones. They're part of something.

I turn back to the computer and see it. I rub my eyes, hoping the reflected sun might have affected my ability to see color. I move closer, lean in toward the monitor. I don't have the spreadsheet sorted properly, but I think there's an extra orange row.

I should search for his ID first, but I sort by color. Oranges first, reds second, colorless rows last. I count the orange rows. I'm right. One new orange ID.

I close my eyes because I know, then open them to confirm. Employee ID 245678 has earned its orange stripe. George has been hurt. Hurt bad.

I should switch to the job board, pull up my template. Post a new job, that's what I should do. But instead, I pace the office. George and I had just eaten dinner together. He couldn't be hurt. He couldn't have gotten back out to sea that quick.

No, I remind myself. That's not what happened. He wasn't there, you don't know his real name. George isn't real. No one on that spreadsheet is real. They're all just numbers. Numbers and colors and positions to be filled if necessary.

"George?" I ask.

He doesn't respond. Of course he doesn't. He's hurt. He's hurt bad enough to turn orange. Any number of things can happen to a man or woman at sea to turn them orange. A near-drowning that permanently disables the brain. A severed limb from a chain or a harpoon to the chest. Some of these things end up killing the person, and when that happens, orange turns red.

Not George, though.

"George, talk to me, please."

I look out the window again. This time, the people outside don't look like they are part of something. They look like they're disparate pieces that can never fit together. That's why I'm in here. I'm part of something. I matter.

"You'll be alright, George. Fight through it. Please."

I sit back down and stare at the spreadsheet. I need to know more. But that's not part of this. My job is to know less than everyone else. My job has purpose and no one else can do it but me.

But I don't want to do my job, I want to know about George.

I open my email in the web browser. I don't check it often. Not much communication flows in from the bosses and none flows out from me. My paystubs are sent there, and six consecutive emailed paystubs appear before my most recent email from the bosses. It was just a note.

"Doing great."

I start a new email. The company directory is nothing but Employee IDs. I wonder if that's how it is for other employees. Or, maybe other employees have a directory of names. Maybe my name is listed among the others in someone else's directory.

I scroll until I find one of the bosses. I find his or her ID and start a new message.

"What do I say, George?" I ask. "Help me with this. I need to know."

I type, erase. Type, erase.

"You're going to be fine. It's OK."

I grab the mouse and move the cursor over the "x" to close the message. I want to click, but I can't. I don't know if George is going to be OK. George is my friend. Friends deserve to know. They deserve to know how the people they care about are doing.

I type again, and this time, the words make their way to the email body. I don't erase. I read the message aloud, to George I imagine.

"Good afternoon," I read. "I know it's not my place to ask, but I'm curious. I would like to know what the medical status of Employee ID 245678 is."

I take a breath. It hurts my lungs. I should erase this message and stop all this. But that's not what I do. I read on.

"I saw his," I say aloud, but then catch myself.

I delete the word "his" and replace it with the words "the employee's" in my email and start reading again.

"I saw the employee's row turn orange, and I wondered what happened. I wondered how serious the injuries are. I understand this is not my place to ask, but I hope that you'll make this one exception. I have done nothing but good work for you, and I'm just asking this once. Will Employee ID 245678 be alright?"

I roll back in my chair, away from the desk and the mouse and the keyboard. Away so I can't send the message. I spin the chair around and think about George. He told me he had a family. I can't imagine his boys growing up without him. His wife, she will be devastated. I need to know.

I shake my head. None of that's real. But it doesn't matter. Real is nothing. The people outside in that shopping center parking lot, they're not real. I'm real. George is real. And I need to know.

I roll forward and lay my hand on the mouse. I move the cursor to the "Send" button and hover there for a moment. Then I click it. It's gone with a whoosh noise from the computer speakers. I close my eyes and wait.

But I don't get a response, and the sun slides across the sky outside my window. The clouds turn orange, and the traffic on the streets around the shopping center picks up. I go to the miniature refrigerator and get another Sprite. I pop it open and chug it.

An hour has gone by. Two. Still, no reply. I haven't posted George's job on the job board.

I go to the computer and look at the spreadsheet. I focus in on George's number. Still orange, as if I thought it would go back to colorless. Once a row is colored, it never goes back.

A car's tires squeal outside my window. I look to the parking lot and see a black van. Two men climb out and walk toward my office. One has a cardboard box in his hands. The other has a manila envelope. They come right up to the door, don't ring the buzzer. They come inside.

"Can I help you?" I ask.

They don't say anything. The one with the box empties the miniature refrigerator of my food and drinks and places it all in the box. He goes to the desk and sweeps all my personal effects into the box. This consists of a single framed photo of my mother and three sharpened pencils.

When he's done, he stands by the door. The other man approaches me. He hands me the envelope and touches my elbow. He nods to the door.

"What?" I ask.

He nods to the envelope, then nods to the door. I open the envelope and find severance paperwork. Three weeks' pay in the form of a check. A letter on Hamilton Fishing Enterprises letterhead explaining that my services are no longer required.

The man who handed me the envelope guides me to the door. Just before we leave, I look back at the computer. Back at the spreadsheet. Back at George's row.

Employee ID 245678's row has turned red.

OUTSOURCING

I stopped being angry months ago. Outsourced it. Made it someone else's problem.

Like, last week—a Monday because of course it was a Monday—when that Subaru brake checked me. Old me would have been out of the car at the next stop light, banging on the motherfucker's glass. That was the old me. That was before I gave up my anger.

My mother used to tell me it took more strength to let something go than to engage with it. "Those words and actions you respond with, they're easy," she'd say. But it never felt easy. Felt like every molecule in my body was bursting, pushing their way outward. Like they wanted to be the ones to react, not me. That didn't feel easy so I'd told her easy was walking away. Easy was pretending like anger wasn't a part of us all.

No, fuck easy. I'd take the hard way because doing the hard thing makes you better. That's what my old man said, at least. "Ain't been a day where a man who worked hard didn't feel pride in choosing the hard thing."

So, I chose the hard thing. All my life, I'd done the hard thing and made myself better for it. If it took my voice, I'd shout until it was gone. If it took my fists, I'd swing until the red and blues lit up the desert. I chose the hard thing. Right up until the hard thing stopped making me better.

Six months ago, on the ridge line of the copper mine I'd grown up hating, Carlos lit into me. Something about an attitude. Something about problems. Something about work ethic and respect. That last one, cutting me across the chest like it'd been the blade of the switchblade I found when I was nine. Respect, he'd said. Like he didn't understand the respect it took to live the way I had lived. To choose the hard thing even when I didn't want to. Even when I'd wake up in the middle of the night crying about what the hard thing meant. Respect. He didn't know what respect meant.

I spent three days in Pima County lockup wondering about those hard things. Thinking about what my mom had said. Promising myself I'd find a way to give up my anger and do the easy thing. Do the lazy thing.

It took a few weeks to figure it out, but the solution had been so easy. So smart. The mining company did it with their accounting. My old man had done it for his landscaping business. My mom even did it for her book club when she'd ask my sister to summarize the book for her because, let's be honest, Mom was never much of a reader.

Outsource my anger. If I didn't have to deal with it, I could have the best of what my mom had told me and what my dad had instilled in me. I could do the hard thing while living the easy thing.

It was perfect. And it was simple.

Anytime someone triggered my anger, I'd blink it away. A flash of white and then it'd be gone. I'd turn around. Leave. But whoever was working my outsourcing contract that day would step in and do the thing that I used to have to do. The words. The fists.

Sometimes, I'd talk to whoever was working my contract. Get the details and shake my head. Couldn't believe it used to be me doing those things. Other times, the stories felt so close, I could feel my knuckles tingling.

Most of the time, I just never knew how it all worked out. Like today when someone asked me about it from across the metal table.

"What's your relationship to Martin Bregswood?"

And.

"We have video."

And.

"We're not asking who, but why."

Then.

"You don't remember?"

I didn't have to remember, though. Because I'd outsourced my anger, and everything was okay now.

THE NOTHING

The headlights lapped at the bean pods lying still across the packed gravel driveway. I pulled the curtain back a little further to get a better look at the truck. With the light coming almost directly at us and the moon getting itself twisted up in the clouds, I could only see the shape. Boxy. Old.

"Go get Dad," I said to my brother, but he didn't move. I turned away from the window, shoved him from the ottoman he'd pulled over next to me. "Go, Danny."

This time, he got up and went to the back bedroom, running his hands along the cracked adobe walls like there wasn't a truck pulling up outside our house. I turned back to the window, let the curtain fall back enough to hide my face, as if that mattered. As the truck came closer, I saw the markings. Painted against the rusted, dented, and chipped door siding was the mark. Three lines up, one across. The fucking mark.

"Samantha, get your ass away from that window and come help me find some guns."

I turned and saw my dad standing with a box of 12-gauge shells in one hand, a flashlight in the other. Danny had the Enfield that my dad promised would fire when we needed it to.

"Why are they here?"

Dad didn't say anything, just turned and went back into the kitchen where he threw open drawers, pulled open cabinets. I turned back to the window.

The truck's lights cut out at the same time as the low rumble of the old engine echoed one last time off our walls and out into the night. In the darkness, the mark seemed brighter. Easier to see. I stared at it, hoping I'd been wrong. Maybe it was a Federale coming by to check up on the gringos. Maybe it was a sheriff from back in Santa Cruz County that got lost and crossed the border south.

Or maybe it was exactly what I knew it was. Terror painted on sheet metal as an announcement more than a warning.

"Sam, if you don't get the fuck in here and find yourself a gun, they'll be taking you back with them."

"Coming," I said, turning away from the window. In the kitchen, I watched Dad load shells into his Remington and Danny play with the trigger on the Enfield.

"Why are they here?"

"I've been telling you, Sam."

"Telling me what?"

"We might not have enough sometime."

I shook my head, slapped at the kitchen table. "Sometime doesn't mean now. Why didn't you tell us?"

My dad stopped messing with the Remington, looked me in the eyes. "Because it's going to be fine. I've got a plan."

I sighed. "Where's Mom?"

"Bedroom," Dad said without looking up from the shotgun.

"With a gun?"

"Hell if I know."

I pushed past my dad, past Danny, went down the hall to the back bedroom. Mom was sitting upright in bed, comforter pulled up to her chin, eyes straight ahead. "It's them."

"I know it is, which is why you need to come out there with us."

She shook her head.

"Well, you need a gun at least."

"No."

"Mom—"

"Your father brought this on us, he can fix it. And if he doesn't fix it, so be it. I don't want a gun, don't want you and Danny with one either."

"That's it? 'So be it'?"

She nodded.

"Then fucking sit here." I left her room, went to my room, and flipped the mattress off my bed and against the wall. Beneath it, wrapped in an old Arizona Wildcats t-shirt on top of the box spring, was the .357 I'd stolen from Margaret's brother before we had to leave Arizona. I picked it up, dropped the shirt, and let my finger rest on the trigger.

Hadn't been cleaned in at least six months—since the last time I'd felt like I needed to use it. Had just three bullets in it.

I stood in the hall, wanting to slap my mother in the face, wanting to shake her until she'd help us. Part of me wanted to leave her back there to fend for herself, but instead, I went to the linen closet. I pulled down the .380 Dad told me never to touch. Used to be his daddy's and he said we'd only ever use that gun in an emergency. I walked to Mom's room, looked her in the eyes, shook my head, then tossed the .380 onto the comforter in front of her.

I went back out into the kitchen and stopped at the table where Dad had dropped an ice chest full of meat. Lid open, smelling like a hundred pounds of roadkill had just been dumped in our house, he counted the individually wrapped packages of steak and ground chuck.

"The smell," Danny said, trying not to look at the meat.

Dad dove his hands in and answered without looking up. "That's what happens when the generator goes out, bud. Been out a day and a half now, so things are going to start to stink."

I stared at the ice chest, thinking about the last time we had anything besides beans and stale cereal. Anything that we could cook over a flame. It should have turned my nose by now, should have sent my stomach to my throat, but I fucking missed the taste of meat no matter what was going on outside our walls.

"What is it?" I asked.

Dad stopped, looked up at me, then looked back down into the ice chest.

"It's not what they want, not human."

"Then it won't work," I said.

"Sam."

"Dad, if it could work, it would have worked already."

"No choice now."

"When were you supposed to deliver?"

"Yesterday."

I shook my head. "You couldn't find anyone this time?"

"No one that wouldn't be missed."

I hated myself for asking, for wishing he'd been able to kill just one more person. My stomach bubbled when I thought about it. Thought about the day my dad told Danny and me what he'd be doing to keep us alive.

"Won't ever be good people," he'd said. "I promise you that."

I closed my eyes for a second, forced everything my dad had ever done from my mind, went to the living room and stopped. Shadows against the curtains. Scraping along the adobe walls outside. Then, a knock.

Quiet, calm. One knock. Then two. I lifted the .357 toward the door, but my dad lowered my arm, looked me in the eyes, and shook his head. He walked across the living room, unarmed, head high, and unlocked the door.

I'd always heard they'd come pounding down someone's door only after a week or more had gone by without a delivery—the ones around here at least, the ones that cared to make deals with us. But I knew they were running short. And I'd never actually met anyone dumb enough to deal with them besides us. Everyone I knew stayed in the States, let the government scoop them up in the draft, fought a war they never wanted to have. The people down here, I didn't know what happened to them. Well, I knew what happened to some of them.

My dad happened.

We were the smart ones. The ones who could buy our way through life. A few pounds of flesh here, a few there. Hand over what was left of people the world would never miss. Serve the community while serving them. That's how Dad had sold it at least. I wasn't sure when he became so comfortable killing people to keep us alive.

Dad pulled open the door. Three of them were there. Skin tight, eyes yellow. But otherwise, human. The hunger hadn't made them any worse. Except for the fact they were at our door after one day of being late on a delivery.

Danny tugged at my free hand from behind me. "Sam."

I ignored him as I watched the three of them standing in our doorway saying nothing to my father.

"Sam," Danny said again, pulling hard on my hand.

I turned and went into the kitchen with him. "What?"

His voice low, Danny said, "Dad told me it'd take more than one shot."

"Yeah?"

"What if they're too fast?"

I shook my head, pointed at the trigger on the Enfield he had cuddled up against his chest like a baby blanket. "Just pull that thing. They aren't any quicker than us."

"But—"

"But nothing. They come at you, pull that trigger over and over again until you're the only one breathing."

By the time I turned back toward the living room, Dad was leading them in. They looked at me as they entered the kitchen, ignored my gun, ignored Danny's gun. They looked at the shotgun on the table, but their eyes jumped to the ice chest like a rock skipping across a pond.

"This is what I got," Dad said.

They leaned over the cooler, flipped the packages of meat back and forth.

"Wasn't easy, either." Dad slid the shotgun off the table while they were busy examining the meat. "You know how many cows are left in Mexico?"

They didn't say anything.

"I heard there's only a hundred and fifty left. A pound of meat costs more than just about anyone has now. This side of the border or north of it."

They tossed the meat back into the cooler and stared at my father, not speaking.

"Look, I'll get you the real thing. Been having trouble finding the right people is all."

They tilted their heads as they looked at me and Danny.

"Come on, you know it doesn't work like that. I'll get you some, but it's going to be the way it's always been."

I wrapped my finger around the trigger of the .357. Three bullets. Three of them.

Danny's voice echoed in my head. *Dad told me it'd take more than one shot.*

Danny was right, and Dad was right. So, I picked the one I'd lay down. The one on the left, taller than the other two. There was no strategy behind it. I just looked and picked, and practiced in my mind.

The one closest to my dad put a hand on his shoulder, pushed him toward one of the chairs around the table, sat him down.

"I told you, I'll get the real stuff."

Dad held the shotgun in his lap as the middle one shoved Danny into a chair, then me. I let him do it while watching the tall one, the top half of his head blowing off in my mind on repeat.

"Dad," Danny said.

"It's okay, buddy. No problem here, right guys?" Dad looked at each of them.

The one closest to Danny sniffed his neck, pointed at him. The others nodded.

I closed my eyes, changed my target. The one by Danny. Three shots to the forehead. Figure out the rest. I opened my eyes and lifted the .357 toward the one standing over Danny. I stood, pressed the barrel to the side of its head.

"Sam, don't," Dad said.

"Get the fuck away from my brother. Take the meat, and walk out that front door."

The other two came around and stood behind me, hands poking at my ribs, noses diving in for quick breaths near my neck. But I held that .357 on the one standing over my brother, waiting for my chance to pull the trigger.

"Sam," Dad warned.

I watched the one hovering over Danny, could feel the shuddering in my brother's bones from across the table. I didn't look at Danny's face because I knew what I'd see, I knew what I'd do. So, I waited, gun out, two of them flanking me like coyotes stalking a stray dog.

After another minute, the one above my brother backed up and looked at the others. Each of them shrugged, then the tall one grabbed the ice chest and lifted it off the table. The three of them walked out of the kitchen, through the living room, and out the front door.

Dad jumped up and ran to the door. I heard him throw it, shut and bolt it. I heard the legs of the chair Danny sat in scrape against the cracked tile floor. I heard Danny's sobs. Then, I felt my dad's arms wrapped around me, his hand pushing my gun hand down.

"They're gone," he said. "It worked."

I shook my head as my dad, Danny, and I sat around the table once more. "It won't work forever."

"I know."

"What're we going to do, Dad?" Danny said.

"We're going to find someone to kill."

"There's no one left," I said. "You knew this was coming, but you made us stay."

Dad set the shotgun on the table, pushed his chair back, stood. As he paced the kitchen, he said, "We don't know and didn't know anything, Samantha. All we've ever been able to do is guess and hope, and that has kept us alive."

"For now."

"Jesus, girl," Dad said. "What do you want from me?"

I sat, head down, flipping the chamber open then closed on the .357. "I want to know why we're here."

Dad stopped pacing. "You know why."

Chamber open, three bullets. Chamber closed. "I know what you told us."

"Sam, we could have stayed and been drafted. Who do you know that didn't get drafted?"

I shrugged, opened the chamber, spun it, closed it.

"You, Danny—you two would have been sent to the wall or maybe out west where it's worse. You want to live your life with a rifle on your shoulder?"

"That's what we're doing now, isn't it?"

"Sam, don't fight," Danny said.

I looked at him and smiled. "I'm not fighting, man, I'm surviving. We all are, and that's different."

"Sam, we're where we are because it's better for us."

I snorted and tossed the .357 onto the table.

"They didn't try anything—"

"Dad, please," I said. "I almost put a bullet in one of them, and if that happened, you know what would have come next."

"Sam," Dad said.

I stood and walked toward the hall but stopped when I heard scraping. Like a tree branch dragged along the back side of our house. "The fuck is that?"

"Watch your mouth, Samantha."

"Listen," I said.

Dad, Danny, and I held our breath. The scraping trailed across the back of the house to the side nearest the kitchen. Past the window over the sink. I ran to it, but Dad pushed me back.

"Don't stick your head near that window."

"I want to know what that is."

"Probably a javelina."

"Dad, what is it?" Danny stood and joined us near the sink.

The sound stopped and we stood in silence for one minute. Two. Three.

"There you go," Dad said. "Wasn't anything."

I turned away from the sink just as there was a single knock on our front door, and I froze. Dad looked at me, looked at Danny, but didn't move.

"Did you ever hear their truck start back up?" I asked.

Another knock at the door.

"Dad!" Danny yelled, pointing at the window over the sink behind us.

Dad and I both spun to find orange flames pecking at the glass like a woodpecker, darkening the window with smoke.

"Shit," Dad said, grabbing the shotgun off the table. He held the gun in one hand then went to the sink and flung open the cabinet door beneath it. He came up with a fire extinguisher.

I watched the flames stretch above the window. Watched them catch on the awning.

Dad didn't bother trying to get outside. He used the bottom of the fire extinguisher to break the window.

The front door split apart at the same time.

I turned and moved toward the living room with the .357 stretched out in front of me. I made a single step into the living room when one of them rushed, shoulder down, into my chest. I fell back across the tile in the kitchen, the gun going off as it slammed into the tile.

I rolled to my stomach, pushed to my knees, and tried to find where the bullet had gone. I ignored the kick to the ribs as I looked for Danny. Please, not him. Please, no.

I found Danny backed up against the sink as the tall one to his left pulled Dad through the window. The errant round had put a hole in the ceiling, not my brother.

I tried to breathe as a kick to the ribs sent me sprawling onto my back. I blinked away pain and saw the third one walking across the kitchen toward Danny.

"Danny, shoot!" I yelled.

I caught the third kick—a dirty boot covering skin that had stretched and dried across muscles that were too taut. I looked up and thought I saw it smile down at me. I swung the .357 up toward its face. The first shot blew a hole in its cheek, but he kept trying to kick. He lunged.

I fired another shot into the top of its head and it collapsed on top of me.

"Dad!" Danny yelled from somewhere to my left.

I pushed the thing off my chest enough for me to shout. "Danny, fucking shoot it!"

I didn't hear a bullet, but I heard a scream. Not Danny's though. My father's.

I pushed out from the dead weight and climbed to my feet. The tall one had Dad by the arm, chewing as Dad tried to punch his way out of its grip.

"Danny," I yelled, crossing the kitchen. "Shoot it."

But Danny stood backed up against the counter, staring the third one in the eyes. I leveled the .357 at the tall one and pulled the trigger.

Nothing.

"Shit!" I tossed the gun down and ran at it, but it threw an elbow into my nose. The crack—the warm liquid on my lips—made the tall one and the one hovering over Danny turn toward me. I tried to look at how bad Dad's arm was before they came for me, but I didn't have time. The tall one leapt and shoved two hands into my chest,. Once again, I was on the floor. The two of them leaned in a few inches away, chomping, chewing at flesh they could already taste. I closed my eyes and waited for it.

The rifle shot blew apart the room.

The air in the kitchen left with the sound. I couldn't breathe. Couldn't see. I pushed at the thing on my chest, its mouth no longer moving. I pushed and kicked and tried to hear. Tried to see. I finally got out from under it, and the sound came back to my ears like I'd opened a door to a concert hall. But I didn't hear music.

I heard screams.

Danny's. My father's.

I blinked away blood that wasn't mine from my eyes and saw the last one—the tall one—tear into Dad's skin. Chewing down to the bone on his hand. The shotgun sat a few feet away on the floor. Danny had the rifle pointed at the tall one, pulling the trigger over and over to the sound of nothing but a dry click. The thing moved its mouth up my Dad's arm, to his neck, searching for fresh meat far from bone.

I dove across the floor for the shotgun, but it saw me. With Dad's neck still in its mouth, it kicked me in the face. This time, my cheek cracked, my eyes blurred. But I slid and grabbed the shotgun in my right hand. As I tried to pull it into my left and steady it for the shot, the tall one let go of my dad and jumped on me. I pushed up with the stock of the shotgun, trying to hold it off. But he was too strong.

His teeth closed in on my face and all I could hear was Danny pulling the trigger on that empty rifle. Click. Click. Click.

A gun blast pierced my ears, and the side of its head blew off. But it kept chomping. I tried to turn my head to find where the shot had come from, but I couldn't move. The tall one, its face half gone, kept chomping.

Then the second shot came.

It was knocked sideways off of me, the top of its head gone. I scrambled backwards, to my feet. I looked down the hall and saw Mom standing there with the .380.

I went to Danny, wrapped him in my arms, kept him from looking at Dad anymore. I reached out for Mom and pulled her into me. I didn't look either, but I heard. I heard the blank space where his breath had been.

I heard the empty. The nothing.

SECONDS

All you have to do is count. That's how you can tell when you've crossed the state line. Feel the car slow down. Feel it stop. Feel the acceleration roll your body against the back of the trunk, and count.

The Border Patrol checkpoint, where the car would slow and stop, is exactly five miles from the California border. They'll drive no faster than the speed limit, which is 70. Do the math. Count it off. Two-hundred and fifty-seven seconds.

He counted because that's all he could do in the three-by-two box he was crammed into. His new skin. The trunk of the old Buick was roomy. That's what his mother always said when they went grocery shopping. That's how it felt when he sat in there, lid up, pretending he was in the cockpit of a fighter jet. But with his knees pulled to his chest, face pressed against the matted and stained fabric, the trunk didn't feel that large at all. His new skin, like his old skin, was tight. Small. Didn't protect him like he thought it should.

He counted because it was easier than remembering the slide, the path that led to his mother slapping him in the face and his father tying his arms behind his back. Counting was easier than wondering if, through the drugs and alcohol, his parents still loved him.

But he did wonder.

He wondered if his mother would enroll him in a school somewhere in California. He wondered if he'd make friends in a new neighborhood. He wondered if his dad would ever throw the football with him again like he did that summer three years ago. Before the pile of cocaine grew as high as a sandcastle on their coffee table, and his father locked that man in the bathroom, and before the two gunshots split apart his ear drums. Before his mother's screaming and the sirens in the distance. He wondered if being in the trunk of that car with his parents on the run meant he was on the run too, or if it meant he was just along for the ride.

Or maybe, it meant that when they came down from their high, he'd still be the only witness to the stupid thing his father had done. And maybe, they'd drive straight to the coast, keep driving until the car was in the ocean. And maybe, they'd climb out of their seats as the water filled the Buick, swim to shore as the trunk bubbled and caved and welcomed the flood.

No, they wouldn't do that, not while he was tucked away inside his new skin.

But he knocked his feet against the trunk, tried to jimmy it open, just in case he could escape and find his old skin. When it didn't budge, he went back to counting. One hundred and thirty-seven seconds until they left Arizona for good, until his mother and father's crime spree went from local to national.

He wished he knew how many seconds he'd have to count off before he found out if they'd ever let him out of that trunk.

Justin Hunter

ABOUT THE AUTHOR

JUSTIN HUNTER grew up in Tucson, AZ, a place famous for tuberculosis and the University of Arizona. He spent most his life trying to escape, but now that he has, he finds himself drawn back in through his writing. He is married to a woman who not only accepts the crazy people living in his head, she actively engages them. His two young boys don't know what they're in for.

Justin received his MFA from Arcadia University. He realized he was a writer at the age of seven when he penned the classic, Jacques Cousteau and the Underwater Robot Octopus. A gold star to anyone who tracks down a copy of that gem.

When he is not writing, Justin is probably doing things that actually pay the bills. He is currently the co-founder of a software company called SimpleID.

Find him on Twitter @polluterofminds.

GRATITUDE & ACKNOWLEDGEMENTS

This book would not have happened if not for the support around me. It starts with my family. My wife, Kaelyn, and my boys, Dean and Casey, have always been so encouraging of my writing.

This particular collection started when I was working on my MFA at Arcadia University. I don't think I ever would have finished this if I had not gone through that program. So, thank you to my professors, Joshua Isard, Stephanie Feldman, and Eric Smith.

And, of course, edits and feedback for each story in this collection were provided by my then-cohort and now-friends. Thank you to Charlie Allison, Tianna Hansen, Vee Clay, Abi Putnam, Nicole Campbell, Julia Richards, and Ashley Fries.

Thank you to these publications for first publishing the following stories from this collection:

Bitterzoet Magazine: "Miracle Mile"
Children, Churches, and Daddies: "Scars"
Corvus Review: "Dirt Roads"; "Shotgun Signs"
Down in the Dirt: "Army Men"
The Drabble: "Strip Mining"
Firefly Magazine: "Not Friends"
Five on Fifth: "The Nothing"
Front Porch Review: "The Dissociative Property"
Ghost Parachute: "Creosote"
The JJ Outré Review: "Jump"
Near to the Knuckle: "Coyote"
Sick Lit Magazine: "Counting Seasons"
Storyland Literary Review: "How to be a Man"
Twisted Sister Lit Magazine: "One Thousand Hours Free"
Typehouse Magazine: "Leaving Arizona